THE GOLDEN CITY

THE GOLDEN CITY

RALPH MILNE FARLEY

ILLUSTRATED BY

VIRGIL FINLAY
AND
SAMUEL CAHAN

STEEGER BOOKS • 2019

PUBLISHING HISTORY

"The Golden City" originally appeared in the May 13, 20, 27, June 3, 10, and 17, 1933 issues of *Argosy* magazine (Vol. 238, No. 3–Vol. 239, No. 2). Copyright © 1933 by The Frank A. Munsey Company. Copyright renewed © 1960 and assigned to Steeger Properties, LLC. All rights reserved. Additional images originally appeared in the December 1942 issue of *Famous Fantastic Mysteries* magazine (Vol. 5, No. 2). Copyright © 1942 by The Frank A. Munsey Company. Copyright renewed © 1969 and assigned to Steeger Properties, LLC. All rights reserved.

"About the Author" originally appeared in the February 22, 1930 issue of *Argosy* magazine (Vol. 210, No. 3). Copyright © 1930 by The Frank A. Munsey Company. Copyright renewed © 1957 and assigned to Steeger Properties, LLC. All rights reserved.

Visit steegerbooks.com for more books like this.

TABLE OF CONTENTS

CHAPTER I

LOST AT SEA

IN MY SCRAP book of epoch-marking newspaper clip-
pings, there is the following from the San Francisco *Chronicle*
of Nov. 9, 1891:

STRANGE MIRAGE SEEN BY WHALER

The harbor is literally strewn with whalers at anchor just now.
There were several fresh arrivals chalked up today.

Late this evening the barque Alaska, of New Bedford, Mass.,
Captain Charles Fisher commanding, arrived with a splendid
catch. She brought 1,400 barrels of oil and 17,000 pounds of
bone, the product of thirteen whales.

Captain Fisher reported a successful cruise with no casualties.
They were, however, becalmed for about a week in mid-Pacific.
At this stage in his narrative to your reporter, a queer expression crossed the good captain's face, as he lowered his voice and
said, " 'Twas then that we saw the golden city." Whereupon he
related the following tale:

On the sixth day of the calm, the Alaska gradually drifted
into sight of an island, finally getting so close that a large city
of Oriental architecture, with golden domes and spires and
minarets, became visible. As the Alaska approached still closer,
it was possible to make out the actual features of the people of
the wharves. The men and the women wore striped blankets and
sandals. Small boats with gaudy-colored sails lay at the wharves.

The Alaska came within a hundred yards of one of the boats.
Captain Fisher hailed them, and blew his fog-horn, but they
took no notice of him. Then suddenly the vision shivered, broke
into pieces and disappeared.

1

"Throw me a rope!" Mayhew shouted

Your reporter, fearing a hoax, separately interviewed at least a dozen members of the crew, and they all told identically the same story, even down to details as to the arrangement of the wharves and the principal streets and buildings, the rigging of the boats, and the costumes of the inhabitants. Either the crew of the Alaska actually saw the same vision, or they have been remarkably well coached.

There is no land charted within a thousand miles of where they saw the golden city, and no known actual city anywhere in the world fits their description of it.

This vision of "The Golden City" was a nine-days-wonder at the time, and it is still remembered and talked about by the sturdy men who sailed the seven seas in those good old days.

Often have I heard the yarn from my uncle, who was a member of the crew of the whaling barque Alaska when it encountered that mirage, or whatever it was. And it is from him that I obtained the above-quoted clipping.

But there was one phase to the episode which, by common agreement of all the crew of the Alaska, was kept from the newspaper reporters. And it is only in very recent years that my aged uncle vouchsafed this particular story even to me.

*Fear followed surprise
on the man's face*

The suppressed item was this: One of the crew, Adams Mayhew by name, was sent aloft to get a better view of the strange land which the ship seemed to be approaching, and fell from a yardarm into the sea when the ship gave a sudden lurch as though it had grounded on a shoal. At that instant the golden city trembled, blurred and vanished; and when the crew of the Alaska, after rubbing their eyes and staring at the empty sea, lowered boats and hunted for their missing shipmate, he, too, appeared to have vanished.

The coincidence seemed so weird and uncanny to the superstitious mariners that they all agreed to say nothing about it. Mayhew was officially reported as having been lost overboard; but how and when was never detailed.

To me it never seemed that there was anything particularly exciting about the loss of Adams Mayhew. In fact I was much more impressed by the absolute inexplicability of a whole shipload of sober, God-fearing New England mariners simultaneously seeing, within easy hailing distance, identically the same mirage of a teeming city, the like of which existed nowhere on the whole surface of the earth! That, to me, was far more important than the fact that one of the crew had fallen overboard in the excitement and been drowned. And yet the awe and horror with which my uncle always spoke of the death of Adams Mayhew caused that episode to stick in my mind.

ONE DAY last summer, as I was hoeing asparagus in the field near the gate of my Chappaquiddick Island farm, a young man with broad shoulders, clear blue eyes and a firm step, and yet with an air of ineffable sadness, came striding down the road from town. He hailed me, and asked me if so-and-so (naming my uncle) lived thereabouts; so I pointed out my uncle's farmhouse, and the stranger strode on.

That evening, after supper and the chores, uncle dropped in on us, as he frequently did. Quite naturally I asked him if the visitor of that afternoon had found him.

"Aye," he replied, "and he tells a sea yarn that would make your hair stand on end."

Said I, "I've always minded to write a sea yarn, as you call it, a tale of whaling adventure, or some such. But from all accounts which you've ever given me, your whaling career must have been pretty humdrum; that is to say, except for the time you saw the vision of the golden city."

My uncle chuckled to himself, and his shrewd old eyes twinkled.

"All right," said he, "this here yarn, which I'm a-telling you, has to do with that golden city. For the caller I had this afternoon is Adams Mayhew, my lost shipmate."

"Well, what of it?" I countered. "There's nothing very exciting, is there, to his having been picked up by some other ship, and having kept it quiet from you folks for all these years?"

"Isn't there, though!" replied my uncle. "You see, Adams Mayhew wasn't picked up until just a few months ago."

"Absurd!" I retorted. "You don't mean to say that he has been floating around in the ocean all these years, do you?"

Then I remembered the apparent youthfulness of the man who had hailed me in the Asparagus patch that afternoon, and I added, "Furthermore, this young man can't possibly be Adams

Mayhew! Why, Mayhew would be nearly seventy, if he were alive today, and this man is still in his twenties."

Uncle's face sobered.

"Yes," he admitted, "that does make it seem a bit peculiar. But Adams claims that he has been gone less than two years. Oh, he's Mayhew, all right. Looks just like he used to, except a bit more filled out. And remembers things which only a member of the crew of the Alaska could possibly know."

"Now look here!" I interrupted. "More likely this is Adams Mayhew's son or grandson, if his name is Mayhew at all."

"Mebbe so, mebbe so," replied my uncle noncommittally. "Anyhow he's staying with me for several days, until he gets his bearings, sort of. Come on over to my house, and listen to his story."

So I did.

CHAPTER II

OVERBOARD

ADAMS MAYHEW'S OWN story tallies with the newspaper report of the vision of the golden city, as quoted above, and also with the whispered account of his having been sent into the tops with a telescope to get a better view of the lay of the land toward which the Alaska was slowly drifting over the hot and oily surface of the Pacific Ocean.

From his perch aloft, Mayhew could see considerably more of the city than from on deck. In the distant background there stood a smoking volcanic mountain. The city itself was certainly one of magnificent gilded buildings and great wealth. Gaily clothed men and women sauntered through its streets. Ornate barges, with gaudy striped triangular sails, were lading and unlading at its docks. Such a short distance away did it lie, and so clear was the air, that the young man could distinguish the individual features of the men and women on the nearest wharves. In fact, he even picked out, with his glass, one young girl as being prettier and more interesting looking than the rest. He hoped that Captain Fisher would dock there overnight, and give all the crew shore-leave.

With these thoughts in mind, Adams Mayhew craned his neck forward and adjusted his telescope to get a better view of the particularly attractive blonde, when suddenly it seemed as though the yard-arm, to which he clung, was abruptly jerked out from under him, precipitating him into the sea.

Mayhew was one of the younger generation of New Bedford

whale-fishermen who had learned how to swim, an accomplishment scorned by his older shipmates. As he dropped through the air he came out of the sprawled position in which he had left his perch aloft, and straightened out to cut the water cleanly with his feet. He even had time to grab hold of his nose with one hand.

As a result of these precautions he was neither stunned nor choked, but he did go pretty deep into the sea. When at last, with sturdy strokes, he reached the surface again, he shook the dripping hair from his eyes and looked around for the Alaska. But the whaling vessel was nowhere to be seen. Adams Mayhew was alone in the middle of the Pacific Ocean.

His first reaction was complete stupefaction and bewilderment, tinged with fear. Then a rational explanation suggested itself: some underwater cataclysm had suddenly destroyed the vessel with all on board, leaving him as the sole survivor. But this explanation wasn't so rational after all, for there had been hardly time for all this to have happened, but at least it was more sensible than to believe that the Alaska had vanished by sheer magic.

And what about the golden city? What had become of it? Mayhew knew perfectly well that the city had been only a mirage. His reason had told him this, even while he had been intently studying its apparent actuality.

Yet, strange to say, although the solid real Alaska had vanished, the mirage still persisted. What good could a phantom city do him in his present predicament?

In spite of a full realization of the futility of the attempt, and cursing himself for a credulous fool, he kicked off his shoes and set out hand over hand toward the nearest dock, which seemed not more than a hundred yards away.

Momentarily expecting the mirage to disappear as he approached it, he nevertheless kept on; and the mirage did not vanish.

When within a few feet of the wharf, Mayhew stopped swimming and surveyed the structure of piles which towered above

*"Once more this pearl of a white girl plays into
our hands," announced the Spider maliciously*

him. Although he knew that it was a mere illusion, it certainly
seemed real enough. Its cool shade felt soothing after his strenuous swim across the oily surface of the tropical sea. The ripples
lapped hollowly at the foot of the timbers. Green seaweed, cling-
ing just below the water-level, sudsed up and down with the
gentle motion of the waves. Mayhew sadly shook his head. All
he had to do was reach out his hand and touch some part of this
mirage, in order to produce much the same effect on it as though
it were a soap-bubble that he was touching.

THEN OF a sudden hope occurred to him: if he were to pierce
the bubble of this mirage, would not that very act of destroying
the unreal restore the real—the barque Alaska, which might
not have sunk after all! At that thought, a panic seized him, a
fear lest the Alaska might at that very moment be silently and
invisibly drifting beyond his reach. All ideas of shore-leaves
with beautiful golden-haired blue-eyed girls left him. He thrust

*Out of the swirling mists which rose from the magic
bowl, there appeared the frightened image of Eleria*

forward one rigid finger against the nearest pile of the wharf, as
though poking at an iridescent film of soapy water.

But the fingertip jabbed painfully against solid wood! The
wharf was real!

Adams Mayhew let out a howl of baffled surprise, which was
instantly echoed by shouts from above. Glancing up, he saw,
peering down over the edge of the wharf, the very unpleasant
face of a young man of about his own age. It was weak chinned,
thin lipped, sharp nosed, vicious, and shifty eyed.

For a moment the two men stared at each other. Mayhew's
face registered hope, and the deference of one about to ask a
favor. But the face above him registered first incredulity, then
surprise, then fear, and finally a smug satisfaction.

It seemed as though the man thought he recognized
Mayhew—as an enemy, a dangerous enemy—but now helpless, and in his clutches. But Mayhew's problem was to get out

of the water. To flee might invite a shower of weapons, whereas to come up unarmed might for the present be the safest course.

So he shouted, "Please lower me a rope."

"Porto!" replied the ferret face. This strange word was followed by a string of utterly unintelligible syllables, in a very peremptory tone of voice. It sounded like a challenge and a threat; and yet there was a note of uncertainty, almost of dread, in it too.

"I'm sorry, but I can't understand you," said Mayhew. *"Parlez-vous Francais? Habla usted Español? Sprechen sie Deutsch? Amenia sabe falar am Portuguez?"* Not that Mayhew could speak any of these languages, except Portuguese; but merely that the answer might give him some clew as to the nationality of these strange people.

The eyes of the man above narrowed suspiciously. His face was withdrawn from view, and he could be heard shouting orders.

Then a rope-ladder was lowered over the side, and Mayhew clambered up with sailorly speed; and soon was standing dripping on the pier, clad in open-necked white shirt, sailor trousers and stockings, in the midst of an inquisitive throng, garbed in gayly striped togas. They seemed to know him—or to think that they knew him. Several of them addressed him, using that same word, "porto," which he had heard from the lips of the man who had looked at him over the edge of the wharf. But Mayhew did not know what to answer, and he merely stared back at them, bewildered.

The prevailing complexions were dark, though some were blond. Most of the men wore square-cut black beards at the tips of their chins, the rest of their faces being smoothly shaven; but some of the younger men had no beards at all. The women all wore their hair in long conical psyche-knots, and wore high waisted Empire gowns, with short puffed sleeves and ruffled skirt bottoms. Both sexes had sandalled feet, and arms covered with golden bands set with jewels and semi-precious stones.

Around the outskirts of the crowd there hung men, and a few

women, of the black, brown and yellow races. Their clothes were simpler and more revealing, and the blacks of both sexes wore nothing above the waist.

DIRECTLY CONFRONTING Mayhew in the midst of the semi-circle of inquisitive humanity which hemmed him in stood the ferret-faced young man, flanked by two Negro hench-men. Although evidently of the prevailing race, he was clad quite differently from the others. Instead of an awning-striped, ground-sweeping toga, draped across the left shoulder, leaving the right arm bare, he wore a simple white, blue-bordered tunic, reaching only to the knees, and gathered in at the waist with a belt from which hung a pouch and a short broad-sword. His cropped curly black hair was bound by a flue fillet.

To do him credit, his face was the only unpleasant part of him, for his body was beautifully proportioned: slim-hipped and broad-shouldered. Mayhew instinctively sized him up, taking mental stock of his own sturdy muscles, toughened by two years of strenuous whale-fishing.

For several minutes the two men surveyed each other. Mayhew endeavoring to appear conciliatory, as befitted a foreigner in a strange land, yet on the alert to defend himself if necessary; his opponent with a truculent sneer on his unprepos-sessing features. In the background could be heard the murmur-ing voices of the crowd and occasionally the word "porto."

Then the man repeated to Mayhew the string of unintelli-gible syllables which he had put to him before. Again Mayhew detected the undercurrent of fear and uncertainty in the man's tone. He appeared to be trying to impress upon Mayhew the fact that Mayhew was at his mercy, and at the same time to get an answer to some question which seemed to be puzzling him.

Mayhew, forgetting that he was among strangers, and for the moment seeing only the single individual who confronted him, blurted out, "I don't know what you're saying, but I don't like your tone of voice."

Evidently the ferret-faced young man didn't like the tone

of Mayhew's voice either. The strange sound of the English language puzzled him, but he quite evidently knew that he was being talked back to. His half-timid, half truculent sneer changed to a scowl of sudden resolution.

Pointing a peremptory finger at Mayhew, he shouted a brief command to the two Negroes. The Negroes converged warily toward Mayhew, each drawing a long scimitar from his waist. Murmurs of disapproval arose from the crowd. Mayhew wheeled and poised on the edge of the dock, preparatory to diving back into the safety of the more hospitable sea.

But he was stayed by the sound of a feminine voice behind him, the most tinkling silvery voice he had ever heard. He gave a swift glance over one shoulder, hoping to catch a glimpse of the face that went with that voice.

It was the golden-haired girl whom he had picked out from the masthead of the Alaska! She had pushed through the crowd and had laid one dainty hand on the arm of her young countryman, and was remonstrating with him. Then she turned and smiled and nodded to Mayhew. The two blacks had ceased their advance and were looking to their master for further instructions. So Mayhew did not dive.

But the young man in the blue-edged tunic was in no mood to be remonstrated with, even by such a pretty and attractive girl. Seizing her hand, he flung it from him with a snarl. The girl stumbled backward into the crowd, with a hurt, bewildered look on her cameo face. Then the young man scouted a curt order to his two minions, and they advanced a second time.

But Mayhew's Yankee chivalry caused him to be filled with rage at the rough treatment which the ferret-faced young man had accorded the girl. With one leap he passed between the advancing blacks and landed on their master. His attack was so unexpected that the man had no time to draw his sword, and the two of them went down together on the wharf.

MAYHEW TRIED to get his hands around the other's throat, but he was cast off. Both men scrambled to their feet. Stooped low, their arms bowed, their fingers spread, they faced each other. Although Mayhew was not quite so strongly built as his opponent, he was no weakling, and catch-as-catch-can fighting had been a daily sport on the Alaska.

Mayhew, intently watching his opponent's face, noted that the man was looking past and beyond him. Sensing danger from behind, he wheeled just in time to see one of the two Negroes in the act of swinging a scimitar down on his unprotected head.

There was no time, and hardly room, to sidestep. To retreat would mean to throw himself into the clutches of the young man with whom he had been fighting. So, with a shout, which momentarily delayed the stroke of the Negro, Mayhew sprang straight at him, beneath the descending blade, and drove his fist with all his force into his bare solar-plexus.

With an agonized grunt the huge black collapsed writhing, his weapon clattering harmlessly to the boards behind its intended victim.

Spinning rapidly around, Mayhew snatched it up and faced the other Negro, who, having seen what had just happened to his mate, had paused irresolute. For a moment they faced each other until finally the black dropped his eyes.

The American took this opportunity to glance quickly around to see what his two other opponents were doing. But too late. For a white arm suddenly shot around his throat from behind, and at the same instant his right wrist was seized by fingers of steel. The sword fell from his nerveless hand. Then a voice by his ear shouted to the Negro to come on.

The black hesitated, however. Mayhew struggled and wrenched, whereupon a knee was placed in the small of his back and the arm across his throat tightened, cutting off his wind.

But a man's voice, a cultured voice, with a ring of authority in it snapped out a sharp command from somewhere near by. Mayhew's opponent muttered something which sounded very much like an oath. The Negro shrugged his shoulders, lowered his blade, and thrust it back into his sash.

Relieved of this menace, Mayhew felt a thrill of exultation. With a sudden accession of strength he twisted around to face his assailant.

HIS RIGHT wrist was still held, and his opponent's left arm was still around his neck, but now it was against the back of his neck, no longer cutting off his wind. He drew in a deep, tortured breath, then drove his left fist straight up at the other's chin.

The jolt separated them. Mayhew wrenched his right hand free. And then, instead of following up his advantage with a right-handed punch, some imp of perverse humor led him to deliver a resounding slap to his opponent's cheek.

Several snickers were heard in the crowd. The ferret face went purple with mortification and rage. The veins stood out on his neck, and with a bellow he charged Mayhew. Mayhew leaped to meet him, and they crashed together and went down once more in a heap.

Several times they rolled over and over, the crowd making way for them. Then Mayhew got his fingers on his opponent's throat, and wriggled astride the man's waist. The man made one frantic effort to push Mayhew away, then with a sudden movement reached for his sword. He got his hand on its hilt, but Mayhew set his knee on the man's wrist, and held off the menace for a moment, meanwhile tightening the clutch of his hands. But the prostrate man was frantic. Slowly he withdrew the blade in spite of Mayhew's knee.

Again the authoritative voice in the crowd boomed forth a command. Mayhew shifted his glance from the man below him to the man who had spoken. The latter was tall, slim, wiry and dark, about fifty years old. An attractive face with a small square black beard at the point of his chin. He wore the prevailing gaudily striped toga.

As Mayhew glanced up, he released one hand from his victim's throat, to ward off the expected stroke from the sword. This gave his opponent just enough leeway. Letting go of his sword, he freed his throat with a thrust of both arms. Then he clutched at Mayhew's throat.

Mayhew threw himself backward to avoid this new attack, whereupon the other wriggled free. Both contestants scrambled to their feet.

For the second time they confronted each other. Both were how panting heavily, and the perspiration was streaming down their faces. As they faced each other thus, the kindly black-bearded man in the crowd stepped forward with a reproving: "Kataka, Kirio," and retrieved the sword.

Mayhew's opponent merely snarled in reply. Then he and Mayhew were at each other again.

This time it was his hands that found Mayhew's throat. And when they fell to the planking together, Mayhew was beneath, with the other sitting securely astride his waist.

Gradually the full realization dawned on the American that there was a real hatred back of this fight. This man evidently thought he recognized Mayhew as some old enemy, some enemy unexpectedly reappeared. What had begun as Mayhew's mere impulsive resentment at the ungentlemanly conduct of the man in the blue-edged tunic, had now developed into a battle to the death.

CHAPTER III

THE "SPIDER"

STRIVE AS HE would, Mayhew could not cast his opponent off, nor free his throat from those mighty hands, nor writhe from beneath the body which sat astride him.

The grip on his throat tightened. The evil face leered down at him, through a growing haze.

Then Mayhew's struggles ceased, and his body went limp. The ferret-faced man drew himself up more erect and swept the crowd with a glance of triumph.

But Mayhew had intentionally gone limp a few seconds in advance of actually passing out. Now with every last ounce of strength that was left in him, he suddenly heaved up one of his legs and hooked it cross the other's face. Then a push with the leg, and his throat was free, as his opponent was forced back and away from him.

For a few moments the man was held thus, until Mayhew got his wind back. But the other, quickly recovering from his surprise, squirmed out from under the leg which held him, and Mayhew, realizing that this move would bring his opponent back on top of him again, threw himself free and sprang to his feet. Up came the other almost simultaneously.

But as the man braced himself for a third charge, Mayhew changed his tactics, and not waiting to get into a wrestling position, leaped in and drove his right fist to the other's jaw.

Down went the man, his skull crashing against the planking as he fell.

Standing astride his prostrate body, Mayhew waited, with clenched fists, for him to rise again.

But all the fight had been knocked out of the man. He opened his eyes, ran one hand bewilderedly across his forehead, then he looked up appealingly at his conqueror.

"Katango," he moaned.

"I suppose that means 'enough' in your language," replied Adams Mayhew, with the trace of a smile on his lips. "Get up!"

Then, suddenly realizing that he was in a foreign land, among strangers presumably hostile, he backed away from the prostrate body, and surveyed the surrounding crowd, alertly and vigilantly. As he cast his eye over the throng, he saw the face of the beautiful yellow-haired girl who had gotten him into this trouble. She smiled at him, and he grinned back at her. By her side there stood the handsome bearded man who had befriended him.

This person stared at Mayhew long and steadily. Then he bent down and whispered something to the girl. She gave a start of surprise, and her pretty face clouded as she replied. The two seemed to be arguing.

Then the bearded man stepped forward out of the surrounding crowd and, placing his right hand on the front of his own left shoulder, bowed slightly. Impelled by a natural politeness and gratitude, Mayhew returned the gesture.

"Tekuo kemel?" the man solicitously inquired.

But Mayhew shook his head.

"I'm sorry," he said, "I can't understand you."

The gentleman stroked his square-cut black beard with one hand, pursed up his lips, and gazed at Mayhew for a moment through narrowed lids. Then he smiled and held out one hand to Mayhew.

"Kom!" said he.

"Now you're talking," replied the young American, taking the proffered hand.

AS THEY were about to leave, the girl with the yellow curls

stepped up to them with a sweet expression of friendliness and welcome in her blue eyes. She placed a slim, dainty, jeweled hand on the wet and begrimed sleeve of Mayhew's shirt and spoke to him in her tinkling silvery voice. Yet it was all in the strange language of these people. The only word which he recognized was "porto," and he still had not the slightest inkling as to the meaning of that word.

He flushed with embarrassment, cast one swift glance at the girl's lovely face, and then lowered his gaze and shifted his feet uneasily. The girl drew back her hand with a gesture of distaste.

The black-bearded man looked from one to the other of them, with pity and understanding in his kind eyes, nodded slightly, then pursed up his lips and shook his head.

"Kom. Porto!" said he, and there was a queer note, an intriguing tone to his deep voice as he spoke the word "porto."

Then this kindly gentleman and the American whom he had taken under his protection began to move away.

The crowd parted to let them pass, and now began to break up. But as Mayhew was leaving with his new friend he glanced around to see what had become of the pretty girl and of his late enemy.

The latter had arisen and was brushing himself off, and smoothing his rumpled tunic. And, to Mayhew's disgust and annoyance, the girl was standing very close to the fellow, talking to him solicitously; almost ostentatiously, it seemed.

Then the black-bearded man led Mayhew through the crowd, and along the wharf. Mayhew felt ill at ease, and very dirty and conspicuous.

At the shore end of the wharf was a stone-paved street, flanked by what appeared to be warehouses. Along this street they passed. No vehicles or beasts of burden were in evidence, but there were large numbers of gayly garbed persons of both sexes and of various races, many of whom stopped to stare at Mayhew as he went by. Some plucked the sleeves of their companions, and even rudely pointed at Mayhew. There were whispered conversations and some laughter, all evidently directed at their strange visitor. Mayhew felt more and more conspicuous and uncomfortable.

Many of these people appeared to be acquaintances of his host, for they greeted that individual with the gesture of the right arm diagonally across the chest, with right hand on left shoulder. To these, the black-bearded man courteously returned the salute. Some even presumed to shout some evidently ribald comment, but these the man silenced with a frown and a peremptory shake of his head. And occasionally the intriguing word "porto" was used; but this seemed to displease the man.

Such was the courtly and assured bearing of his new friend, Mayhew soon got over his embarrassment and timidity, until finally he held his head proudly erect—despite his strange and dripping garments—and strode along beside his host as an equal. The man, noticing this, smiled and nodded approval.

Thus they passed on, up the street of the warehouses, until they came to a large public square, around which were grouped ornate and towering buildings of carved marble, chased with gold, and capped with domes and towers and minarets all tiled with that precious metal. Mayhew forgot the staring multitudes and his own uncouth appearance in his awe and wonder at the scene.

AS THE young American stood staring about, he suddenly noticed that something across the plaza had attracted the attention of his benefactor. A crowd was gathering in front of one of the buildings, an excited crowd, that gesticulated and pointed at something in their midst. Down the various streets, which converged at this public square, many people came running, to swell the crowd. And thither Mayhew's bearded friend now made his stately way, followed by Mayhew.

As they reached the outskirts of the jostling throng, someone shouted: "Julo!" and the crowd made way for them. And so Mayhew was able to see what it was that had caused all this commotion. It was a bulletin board on the face of the building;

and on the board was posted what appeared to be a handbill or notice, written or printed in characters resembling Egyptian or Chinese. But the outstanding feature of this poster was its heading: a picture of a huge, fat, repulsive, black spider!

The moment the eyes of the bearded gentleman fell upon the poster his handsome face contracted into a scowl. As he read on his jaw became set and his hands clenched. Finally he wheeled around, and wrapping his toga majestically about him, he stalked out of the crowd like a thunder-cloud of wrath.

Of course, Mayhew hadn't the slightest idea what it was all about. The spider-heading on the poster had somehow cast a chill over him; but, beyond that, the poster had conveyed nothing. So, with a puzzled frown, he ran his fingers through his sandy hair and followed his patron across the public square.

The streets which radiated from this plaza were flanked with lesser buildings of much the same architectural style, and up one of these streets for several blocks the stately, bearded man continued his slow and dignified march, his face softening as he progressed. Finally he halted before a doorway a bit more elaborate and gold-encrusted than the rest.

"Ya," said he, indicating the place with a lordly wave of his hand, a slight inclination of the head, and a friendly showing of white teeth.

But suddenly he recoiled from the door and clutched his toga in front of his throat as he stared aghast at what he saw before him. Adams Mayhew looked at the door, to see what it could be that caused his friend this consternation.

It was a small piece of paper or parchment; and imprinted upon it was a black spider, exactly like the one at the top of the notice in the plaza. Only that, and nothing more.

Mayhew turned his glance from the spider to the face of his friend. It was ashen.

But as he looked, the man regained a measure of his composure. With a determined shake of the head he stepped forward, ripped the offending piece of paper from its place, tore it into little bits, and scattered them in the street.

Then, his face once more serene, he pointed to the scattered bits, placed his finger on his lips, and looked fixedly at Mayhew.

Mayhew nodded. He understood the gesture of silence, even though everything else about the occurrence had been a mystery to him.

His host, satisfied, rapped three times with a golden knocker which hung from one of a pair of carved, golden doors. The doors swung open at the sound, and two black men, naked to the waist, bowed low within the entrance.

With a slight inclination of the head, the man bade Mayhew enter.

The doorway led into a spacious, golden-pillared hall, down which there approached a young-faced, though white-haired, woman in a maroon gown.

Her face wore a puzzled expression as she drew near, and she uttered an explanation coupled with that mysterious word, "porto."

But her husband—for it was evident that she was the wife of the man with the small black beard—hurriedly spoke several sentences, which were evidently some sort of an explanation relating to Adams Mayhew. She paused, clasped her hands with an involuntary little gesture, wrinkled up her forehead, and said:

"Oh!"

But what she had thought, or what was the purport of the man's explanation, or what she thought now, Mayhew could not even guess.

On the chance that it was the correct thing to do, he placed his right forearm diagonally across his chest and bowed low.

Then her husband, with a word of excuse to Mayhew, drew her aside for a moment, and they conversed together in low tones. At the conclusion of their conference, they turned their guest over to one of the black male servants, who—grinning broadly—led Mayhew away.

DOWN THE ornate hallway they passed, into a flower-filled court, and thence by an outdoor staircase to a second story balcony, and what evidently was a sleeping apartment. Here the black man signaled to Mayhew to remain, and then withdrew. Mayhew sat down gingerly on the edge of a gaudy divan.

Soon the black servant returned, bearing a kimono-like robe of flowered crepe material which he handed to Mayhew, who slipped off his dripping sailor clothes and put on the gaudy bath-wrap.

Then the Negro led him to a large room of glazed figured tiles, depicting scenes evidently of the golden city and the surrounding country. In the background of one of the pictures, the volcano which Mayhew had seen from the Alaska hung ominous and menacing, surmounted by a black pall of smoke. Somehow it fascinated the young American. The shape of the mass of smoke was vaguely reminiscent of the sign of the spider which had caused so much excitement that afternoon.

In the middle of the tiled room there was a sunken swimming pool, and along the walls there were marble benches, and cubicles containing showers.

The young whaler had never seen either a shower bath or a swimming pool; but his attendant, with a very puzzled expression on his shiny ebony face, demonstrated their use.

On his return to his own room, Mayhew found that during his absence his wet and dirty clothes had been removed. On the couch lay, a blue and white striped toga, a sleeveless undershirt, a strip of white cheese-cloth, several feet of blue ribbon, and some jeweled bracelets and armlets and clasp-pins. Mayhew put on the undershirt, and the Negro showed him how to wrap the white cloth around his waist to form a crude undergarment, how to don the striped toga, and how to tie the fillet in his hair. He rebelled, somewhat at the fillet, and positively refused the ornate jewelry.

When finally dressed, he surveyed himself in a mirror, and

was surprised to see how completely he looked a native of these parts. Then his attendant led him back to his host and hostess.

Both of them gave a start of surprise as he entered, and Marta, as her husband called the woman, could be heard to whisper: "Porto?" inquiringly to her husband. But the man shook his head with an amused and quizzical smile, and advanced to greet Mayhew with extended hand.

Then the host led the guest into a small adjoining room, in one corner of which there stood a large globe of the world, mounted on a tripod. Here at last was something which might furnish the key to all these mysteries! With a glad "Ah!" Mayhew stepped over to it.

But it bore no map of the earth like any he had ever seen before. True, there were continents which vaguely resembled North and South America, Europe, Asia, Africa and Australia. But the Gulf of Mexico extended northward in a narrow V until it joined the Great Lakes, and there was a second group of lakes apparently in the midst of the Rockies. Siberia was connected to Alaska by a narrow band of land. The Mediterranean Sea was an inland lake. A large island lay in the south Atlantic, almost touching the northern tip of Africa. And the Pacific was filled with three parallel, almost adjacent continents, stretching from east to west.

CHAPTER IV

THE LOST CONTINENT

THIS WAS NOT the earth! It was some travesty on the earth. Perhaps a strange planet! Mayhew rubbed his eyes and brushed his hand across his troubled forehead.

Then he swept his arm around him to indicate the surrounding city and pointed to the globe. His host instantly caught his meaning, and indicated the north-eastern corner of the northerly one of the three Pacific continents. Mayhew studied the location. Yes, that would be just about the latitude and longitude of the Alaska when he was last aboard her.

He pointed to the island which lay in mid-Atlantic.

"Atlantis," replied his host.

Mayhew had never heard of any such place.

So he pointed inquiringly to the land of his present location.

"Mu," replied his host. "Ra Mu. Ulu-umil Ra."

Quite a mouthful! Mayhew could not be sure how much of that was the name of the place, and how much was description or explanation.

South America, the man designated as "Xibalba." But as to North America, he shook his head and shrugged his shoulders; apparently the place had no name.

Then Mayhew pointed to himself and to the north Atlantic seacoast, but his host shook his head incredulously. Apparently it was inconceivable to him that any one could live on the continent that had no name.

Their geographical conference was interrupted by the entrance of one of the Negro servants with a message for Mayhew's host, who at once left the room, signaling to his guest to follow him.

In the great hallway there stood the beautiful girl of that afternoon's encounter on the pier, now in earnest conversation with the hostess. As Mayhew entered with his host, the girl looked up, gave a start and blushed, then held her head high and turned away.

Mayhew put his arm diagonally across his chest and bowed to the two ladies. But the girl ignored him. Instead of looking at Mayhew, she turned to the host, addressed him as "Julo," and in an undertone asked him a question which included that ever-present word "porto."

But Julo shook his black-bearded head, and his eyes twinkled mischievously.

"No, Eleria," he said, then spoke a string of unintelligible syllables.

The girl and he disputed for several minutes. Then she bade good-by to Julo and Marta, and left without even a glance at the luckless Adams Mayhew.

She had been gone only a few minutes, when there was a commotion at the door, and the ferret-faced young man Mayhew had fought that afternoon at the wharves forced his way in at the head of a squad of rough looking individuals, garbed like him in blue-bordered tunics, and like him armed with broadswords.

As the leader of the intruders saw Mayhew he stopped, and his jaw dropped with surprise at Mayhew's new clothes.

Then, pointing his finger, he shouted, "Porto!" and sprang forward, followed by his men.

But Julo, the host, stepped between them. Calmly and author-itatively, but with flashing eyes, he addressed the young centu-rion, until apologetically the latter withdrew at the head of his cohorts. But, as he left, he flashed a look of hate at Adams Mayhew, and shouted at him a string of words, ending in the mysterious epithet, "porto."

Not understanding what was said, Mayhew could merely

shrug his shoulders, and make the Muian gesture of hand on shoulder, at his departing enemy. His gesture was met with a sneer. Then the man was gone.

Julo turned on Mayhew with an expression of supreme contempt on his handsome aquiline face. It was the first look other than one of courteous gentlemanliness that he had ever given his guest. Then his expression softened and changed to understanding and mild amusement.

Dinner followed soon after, served in elaborate style from utensils of solid gold. Julo at once set about teaching Mayhew the language of Mu.

Finally Mayhew was escorted off to bed by the huge Negro who had been assigned to him. His host and hostess accompanied him as far as the courtyard and there bade him goodnight.

SLEEP CAME quickly to the tired young man. And as quickly came a sudden awakening in the middle of the night.

His first reaction was to miss the accustomed roll and toss of the barque Alaska. Vaguely he wondered if the vessel had made port, or if it were drifting on an unusually calm sea. Then in a flash he remembered that he was ashore on the mirage-continent of Mu, in the house of the kindly Julo, who had befriended him. He turned and stretched himself on the luxurious sleeping couch, then stiffened to alertness as he heard a slight scraping sound in the courtyard below.

It was not much of a sound. On board ship, it would have passed as the momentary rattle of a bit of tackle. On shore, back in New Bedford, it might have been an alley-cat, or the scuffing of a pebble by the foot of a late passer-by. But here in this quiet household the sound, slight though it was, was out of place.

Springing noiselessly to his feet, Mayhew crept through the doorway of his room out onto the second story balcony which overhung the courtyard. The rays of the moon, coming over the house-wall above him, flooded the opposite side of the court, and thence diffused their light throughout the entire inclosure.

*Sometimes real flames
would leap upward
and lap the rock where
Mayhew stood, driving
him back against the
sharp points of the
spears behind him*

Near the middle of the court, shaded from this reflected light
by a bush, crouched a black form.

As Mayhew watched, the figure slunk forward. There was
something indefinably Oriental about it, and in one hand it
held a dagger. It was headed for the doorway through which
Mayhew had seen his host and hostess withdraw after bidding
him good-night.

His first impulse was to warn the household. But instantly he realized that the only certain effect of a shout for help would be to put the prowler on his guard. Doubtless servants would come running, but the intruder was by now only a few paces from the door of Julo and Marta, and might easily be able to reach his victims before aid could arrive.

So, catlike, Mayhew raced around the balcony to a position just above the assassin, and then as silently clambered over the edge of the railing, and slid down one of the posts.

As his feet struck the ground, the man, with hand already on the latch of Julo's door, heard him and wheeled. Then the two of them launched themselves at each other.

Mayhew caught the wrist of the upraised dagger-arm of his adversary with both his own hands, and thrust his right elbow beneath the other's chin. A wrench of his powerful fingers, and the poniard clattered to the tiles. Then the other's free hand was at Mayhew's throat.

"Help!" shouted Mayhew. "Murder! Help!"

Although these words were in English, the tone of voice meant "help" in any language. Doors opened. Foot-steps sounded on the tiles of the court, and on the balcony above.

Then a cloud passed across the face of the moon, and the whole inclosure became suddenly and ominously dark.

Mayhew's assailant was jerked away from him by unseen hands. Other unseen hands seized Mayhew and pinioned his arms. Warm smelly human bodies engulfed him. And over all could be heard the babel of shouts in a strange tongue.

Then the clangor of a gong. Then lights. Mayhew suddenly found that he was no longer pinned down. He scrambled dazedly to his feet.

Silhouetted in the doorway of Julo's sleeping apartment stood Julo himself, with toga hastily draped across his shoulders, and a lantern in his hand. Six or eight huge Negroes stood about Mayhew, staring at him and at Julo and at each other, with surprise and confusion on their black features.

Julo snapped out a question. Several of the servants, with

much shrugging of the shoulders, began to explain; but their master silenced them, and pointed a forefinger at Mayhew, with a sadly accusatory expression on his handsome face.

What could Mayhew say, not knowing more than a few words of the language! He could at least try signs and pantomime.

So he pointed to the gallery by his own bedroom door, and then to himself. Julo nodded. Then Mayhew pointed to his own eyes, and to the center of the courtyard. Julo nodded again.

Then Mayhew pointed to the bush, by the side of which he had first seen the prowler; and, going over to it, crouched beside it, and began sneaking toward Julo's door. Julo stopped him with a peremptory gesture, and shot a question at the Negroes. But they shook their heads, and shrugged their shoulders.

Back toward Mayhew, Julo turned, with a frown on his handsome face, and moistened his lips with the tip of his tongue. But, just as he was about to speak there came a shout from the shadows in a far corner of the courtyard, and every one crowded over with lights to see what it was about.

It was the dead body of one of the Negro servants, lying on its back with a dagger through its heart! And, pinned to the breast by the weapon there was a piece of parchment bearing the sprawled figure of a loathsome black spider!

All stared at it for one long moment. Then Julo set down his lantern, walked over to Adams Mayhew, placed his left palm on the young man's shoulder and warmly shook his right hand.

Of the mob of assailants who had invaded Julo's house, there was not a sign, but for the rest of the night a Negro servant stood guard in the middle of the courtyard, and one slept in front of Julo's door, and one in front of Adams Mayhew's.

WITH DAYLIGHT, the household took up its usual routine. Everything seemed so peaceful and serene that Mayhew began to doubt if the events of the night before had not been merely a dream.

His language lessons progressed, under the tutoring of his genial host and hostess. But when he sketched upon a piece of paper the rough figure of a spider, and asked the name for it, Marta clutched at her heart and hurriedly left the room; and Julo, with a sudden scowl, seized the paper and tore it into little bits. Mayhew apologized—in English, of course.

Shortly before noon Julo gathered his household together and led them from the house, he and Marta and Mayhew clad in brilliant togas, and the blacks naked to the waist, with baggy pantaloons, and scimitars in their sashes. An air of alert tenseness pervaded the group, but they reached the public square without any untoward event.

Ascending the steps of one of the buildings with his retinue, Julo knocked on the door. It was opened by a white-bearded old man in a flowing yellow robe, with a flaming red swastika emblazoned upon its left breast. He and Julo exchanged a few sentences, and the party was admitted.

Never had Mayhew seen so much gold; the entire interior of the building was literally encrusted with it. The party passed through rooms of increasing brilliance, until they came out into a huge amphitheater. The whole was made of white marble, every inch of which was covered with ingeniously carved gold fretwork. Around the walls ran tier after tier of marble seats, surmounted by a canopy of fluted gold, supported on spiral golden pillars. But beyond this canopy the room had no roof, being completely open to the sky. In the exact center of the amphitheater stood a square altar of unadorned white marble.

Some of the seats were already occupied. Julo and his party were shown to places, and seated themselves. Other persons came in, until the place was nearly filled.

A few minutes before noon a bell sounded, and all conversation ceased. Then, through a doorway beneath the stands, a procession of yellow-robed priests entered the arena. They filed once around the circuit, then the leaders advanced to the center with golden baskets containing wood and tinder and incense, which they piled upon the altar. Then all except the high priest ranged themselves along the wall at the foot of the stands.

The high priest, kneeling beside the altar and raising his hands aloft toward the sun, began to intone a chant. Mayhew could make out none of the words, except the oft-repeated syllable, "Ra," which he had learned was the name of the sun.

As the priest ceased his chant, an even deeper hush settled over the audience. Then there came a flash, like lightning from the cloudless sky, and the pile on the altar blazed up.

A sigh, as of relief, passed through the crowd.

"Doubtless some easily explainable trick," thought the American, "but these people accept it as magic from their god."

A TINY cloud passed across the face of Ra, the sun; the fire began to smoke; a tenseness came over the crowd; and in that instant a cry of mortal agony rang out, as one of the circle of priests who lined the wall of the arena pitched forward on his face.

The hilt of a dagger protruded from his back, pinning to him a small piece of parchment, bearing the dread insigne of the spider! That, and nothing more.

Yet no one had been standing behind the stricken priest!

For an instant the near-by throng recoiled from their dead comrade. Then, at the command from the high priest, they picked up the body and hurried it to the altar. Sweeping aside the now smoldering sacrificial fire, the officiating prelate directed the gentle removal of the knife, and the placing of the dead body, face up, upon the altar. The sign of the spider he tore into small pieces and trod under foot. Then began a second chant to Ra, the sun, who by now had reappeared from the cloud.

To Adams Mayhew the entire performance was merely a part of the temple ritual, the worship of the sun god of these people, culminating in human sacrifice. How revolting! He marveled that a person of the evident intelligence and culture of Julo, his host, who had exhibited such repugnance at the spider-topped poster in the public square, and at the spider-marked piece of parchment plastered on his own front door, should nevertheless be driven by his superstitions or his religious fanaticism to attend temple services dedicated to the thing which he abhorred.

Mayhew glanced apprehensively about him and noted that Marta's face was white and quivering, and that Julo's black-bearded jaw was firm and set, and that the black guards, with drawn scimitars, were standing around the three of them in hollow-square formation, facing protectively outward. But perhaps this, too, was all a part of the ritual.

Then Mayhew remembered last night's fighting in the court-yard, and the Negro who had been found dead there, with the mark of the spider upon him. Surely a man's own religion would not creep into his household in the dead of night to commit assassination. Much perplexed, Adams Mayhew turned his attention back to the arena below him.

The high priest was still praying to Ra, the sun; and he seemed to be putting into his words much more sincerity and depth of feeling than he had put into the original chant which had accompanied the lighting of the sacrificial fire.

As the aged prelate prayed, the body on the altar stirred slightly; whereupon all the priests burst into a joyous hymn of praise, and two of their number rushed forward to the center and bore their stricken comrade tenderly away. Then every one, including the audience, knelt in silent prayer.

The tension appeared to have been greatly relaxed.

If this was all mere ritual, it was well acted!

ON THE return of the party to the house of Julo, Mayhew's language lessons were resumed. Nothing further of excitement happened, although—or perhaps because—guards were posted every night in the courtyard, and no member of the household ever went out in the streets unescorted. Moorfi, the huge black man who had been assigned to Mayhew on the day of his arrival, always slept on the balcony just outside his door.

Marta became increasingly nervous in Mayhew's presence, and treated him as though he were an insane person who must be carefully coddled, lest he break loose and do violent damage.

But Julo still displayed confidence in him, and regarded him with an amused and whimsical tolerance.

Naturally Mayhew was most anxious to return to America at the earliest possible moment, but in this desire he was unable to evoke any cooperation or even sympathy from his otherwise kind and considerate host, who absolutely refused to believe that any civilized people inhabited that barren and desolate continent, although he accepted Mayhew's announcement of his name. "Adamo Mayho" was as near as he could come to pronouncing it, however. Mayhew finally gave up the attempt to interest his host in the proposition of return, merely resolving that at some later date he would try to find passage home on some one of the many trading vessels which made port at this Golden City. And perhaps the presence here of the yellow-haired Eleria may have had something to do with dimming his eagerness to return home.

As the young American rapidly mastered the language of Mu, many of the matters which had puzzled him were cleared up. But many more were not.

For example, he learned that the island, or continent, on which he was located was known as "Mu" or "Ra Mu," "Ra" being the name of the sun, or sun-god, whom these people worshipped. Mu claimed to rule the entire world, which was known as "Ulu-umil Ra"; that is to say, the empire of the Sun.

Also he learned a little, but not much, about "the spider." The people of Mu did not know much about this creature themselves, except that he was supposed to be the head of a secret organization of some sort, which was bent on world domination. None of his followers had ever been apprehended. His whereabouts were unknown. Whoever attempted to thwart him was marked for slaughter.

The spider's demand for tentative recognition and a parley, posted in public squares on the day of Mayhew's coming, had been the culmination of a series of acts of terrorism. Julo had been leading and directing the investigation of the spider's activities. Hence the marking of Julo's door, and the midnight attempt to assassinate him.

IN SPITE of the rapid progress Mayhew made in learning the language of Mu, there was one word the meaning of which kept eluding him, namely the word "porto." Apparently it was the name for something which he resembled. Also, because the mention of it always appeared to embarrass his hostess, he deduced that it was an uncomplimentary epithet; and so at a very early stage of his language lessons he gave up asking even his host about the word.

This was most unfortunate, as events later turned out; for a knowledge of the meaning of that word "porto" might have saved him considerable discomfort and even danger.

But, although many matters appeared inexplicable, he did learn something about his host and his enemy, and the positions which they occupied in the community. Julo was a magistrate of some sort, a person high in the councils of the city. Tirio was a centurion of the police, rather dissolute, and quite a leader among the younger set. Also suspected of plotting against the government. A trouble maker and discontent-spreader. Although he did not come directly under the jurisdiction of the magistrate Julo, he stood in considerable awe of him. Tirio hated and feared Julo, much as a jackal hates and fears a lion. Most of this, Mayhew learned from the faithful Moorfi.

In fact, Mayhew learned a great deal from Moorfi, who was a most garrulous and entertaining Negro, with an effervescent sense of humor and doglike loyalty.

Not all of Mayhew's time was spent indoors, nor even in the courtyard of Julo's house. Once or twice each day he explored the Golden City, sometimes accompanied by his host. Always, regardless whether or not Julo was with him, he was followed by Moorfi and one or two other blacks. Moorfi had been assigned as his personal body-servant, and had developed quite an attachment for him.

On these walks Mayhew never happened to run across the

ferret-faced Tirio; but twice he met the beautiful golden-haired girl, Eleria, and each time she ignored him completely. Just why she acted this way, he could not imagine. Her coolness and disdain were even more inexplicable than Tirio's hatred.

One afternoon, Mayhew and Moorfi were strolling along together through an unfrequented part of the city, followed by another huge black, a new-comer in the household of Julo. Moorfi was in the midst of telling Adams Mayhew a rather long and involved funny story about two traveling merchants, when suddenly a door was flung open just abreast of them, and four burly ruffians, garbed in the blue-bordered white tunics of the police swarmed out upon them, with broadswords in their hands.

CHAPTER V

KIDNAPED

ALTHOUGH TAKEN COMPLETELY by surprise, Moorfi was not in the least nonplussed. With one sweep of his left hand he thrust his master behind him, at the same instant drawing his scimitar and barring the way to the aggressors. The muscles of his bare brawny back and shoulders rippled with alert excitement.

Here, then, at last was the menace for which Mayhew had been tensely awaiting all these weeks. Here was the justification for the vigilance with which he and the other members of Julo's household had been guarded. The Spider had struck again.

Mayhew itched to get into the fight himself, for these thugs were evidently minions of that public enemy, the Spider; but unfortunately he was unarmed. So he turned, to urge the other black into the fray. But, to his surprise, he saw that he was standing irresolute, with his scimitar still in the sash of his pantaloons.

"Come on! Help, Moorfi!" shouted Mayhew. "What are you afraid of?"

But still the black did not stir, and there was a strange gleam in his eye that Mayhew did not like. Moorfi, warding off the attack of four blades, was falling back toward Mayhew and the other Negro.

"Here, give *me* your sword, if you're a coward!" exclaimed the young American, exasperated, as he reached for it.

But, with a quick and unexpected movement, the Negro suddenly clouted him on the side of the head with one huge hand, sending him reeling against the building. Then the black man drew his scimitar and leaped at Moorfi's unprotected back.

"Kataka, Moorfi!" shouted Mayhew.

With the lithe grace of a black panther, Moorfi wheeled, and met the descending blade with a sweep of his own.

Mayhew staggered to his feet. But his view of the fight between Moorfi and the other Negro was now cut off by the four thugs, who all pounced on him as he rose. He drove out his fist at the foremost and then went down again, with the four on top of him.

For a few moments he struggled, but his adversaries proved too much for him. His striped toga was yanked off of him, torn into strips and used to bind him. When the four thugs finally arose, Mayhew's ankles had been strapped together, his elbows bound behind his back, and his mouth gagged.

In the street in front of him lay the slashed and carved carcass of a huge Negro. Over the prostrate form stood Moorfi, his broad back gleaming with perspiration, and a red and dripping scimitar in one clenched fist. Unconcernedly he stooped and wiped his blade on the baggy pantaloons of his fallen victim, then picked up the other's scimitar from where it lay unreddened on the paving stones of the street and turned majestically, with a weapon in each hand, to face the four thugs.

Flashing one brief glance at Adams Mayhew, he addressed them, saying, "Well, I have disposed of his guard, and am at your service, gentlemen."

Mayhew gasped in amazement at this display of faithlessness on the part of his supposedly devoted Moorfi. Even the four bruisers appeared to be a bit flabbergasted at this latest development. They shifted their feet uncertainly.

One said, "But isn't this fellow the one who tried to defend this 'porto' from us, when we first attacked him?"

"I think not," replied another.

"I'm sure that the *dead* Negro is one who resisted us," said the third. "I remember this fellow springing to help us."

"Well," remarked the fourth, "all Negroes look alike to me. Let's not take any chance of his being the wrong one."

But the third thug spoke up again authoritatively, "Captain Tirio told us that he had planted one of his own servants in Julo's household to help us with the kidnaping. And didn't this black man lead our victim right here to the appointed spot at the appointed hour?"

At this mention of Captain Tirio, Mayhew gave a start. He had thought that the attackers had represented the mythical Spider, and now they turned out to be merely minions of Tirio. Then a new idea occurred to him; perhaps they represented *both* Tirio and the Spider; perhaps those two were allies!

Meanwhile one of the thugs was asking Moorfi, "What is your name, fellow?"

"Tuggi," replied the black man without hesitation. "Tuggi, of the household of Tirio."

"There! You see—"

"Quick!" interrupted another of the thugs. "Some one is coming down the street. Here you, guard the corpse. I go to headquarters to report finding it. The rest of you, into the house with the prisoner!"

THE HUGE black man slid his two scimitars into his sash, and effortlessly lifted the trussed-up Adams Mayhew in his arms. As they passed into the house through the still open door with two of their captors, he whispered hurriedly in the ear of the young American, "Courage, master; it is all for the best. We may learn something by getting inside their house; and I could not attack them while you were bound."

The door closed behind them. They stood in a dimly lit corridor.

"Where shall I put the prisoner?" asked the Negro.

"Set him down here," replied one of the thugs, "while I go to report to Captain Tirio."

*Mayhew lurched
over the edge of
the fire-pit*

"Just a minute," interposed Moorfi, lowering his human burden to the floor.

Then as the departing man paused and turned expectantly, Moorfi leaped, and swung at him with his scimitar. The blade caught the man on the side of his neck and he went down with a gurgling groan.

"Surrender, in the name of the magistrate Julo," hissed Moorfi, turning on the other thug.

But, no coward, the other drew his short broadsword and rushed in, too close to be reached by the longer weapon of the Negro, at the same time calling loudly for help.

The noise of many approaching footsteps could be heard.

Moorfi dropped his scimitar, seized the wrist of the sword-hand of his assailant, and closed with him.

The scimitar thudded point downward to the floor and stuck there humming, within a few inches of Mayhew's feet, its edge toward him. In an instant he had thrust his feet against it, thus severing the strip of cloth which bound his ankles. Then backing around, he freed his elbows.

Without waiting to untie the gag about his mouth he

snatched up the scimitar and drove it into the body of the man who was grappling with the Negro.

As the man collapsed, Mayhew tried to shout, "Quick, Moorfi, the door!" But all that came was a stifled grunt.

Then a throng of armed men bore down upon them from the corridor. Moorfi drew his remaining scimitar and side by side the two friends, black man and white, with their backs against the door, fought against the oncoming horde.

As Mayhew battled in the dimly lit corridor, he heard a familiar voice beyond and behind the throng of enemies, shouting, "Don't injure the prisoner. He must be captured unscathed."

Then some heavy object, hurtling through the air, struck him on the forehead and he knew no more.

WHEN HE regained consciousness he was being carried hurriedly through the house. His ankles had again been tied together, and his elbows again were securely pinioned behind his back. His head ached terribly, and his ears hummed.

Through the confusion of his senses, he heard the voice of Tirio exclaiming, "The curse of Ra upon you! Why did you let the black man escape? Now he will warn Julo, and we'll have the whole town upon us!"

So the faithful Moorfi was safe! Adams Mayhew heaved a sigh of relief. Then his head swam and a black fog engulfed him.

When he awoke it was night. He was lying, still bound and gagged, on a rough mattress which swayed gently up and down. His head throbbed dully. Around him he could hear the hum of voices, the lap-lapping of water and the rhythmic dip of oars. Overhead the stars shone. An intermittent warm breeze brought to his nostrils the sweet exotic scent of some pungent flower.

Mayhew felt unutterably tired, and drifted off to sleep.

The next thing he knew, he was lying on the stone floor of a small stone-walled room. He felt dizzy and bruised and battered. For a few moments he just lay and stared dully about him. Then he vaguely tried to remember who he was and how he had gotten here.

He was Adams Mayhew, of the crew of the whaling barque Alaska. That much was clear.

Then events began slowly to piece themselves together in his mind. The mirage. His fall overboard from the Alaska. The girl, Eleria. The rat-faced Tirio. The fight on the wharves. The kindly Julo, and his wife Marta. The faithful Moorfi. The various manifestations of the Spider, whoever that might be.

As his mind cleared, events came back to him more rapidly. He was the guest of Julo, magistrate of one of the seven cities of Mu. There had been a fight in the streets and he had been kidnaped.

He stretched his arms and felt of his bruised muscles; thus he noticed that he was no longer bound. He ran his fingers perplexedly through his sandy hair. He coughed, and noticed that he was no longer gagged.

Then he got unsteadily to his feet. His striped toga was gone and he was clad only in undershirt, waist-cloth, and sandals. He felt stiff and cold.

When he had stretched his cramped limbs and had slapped himself warm again he began to examine his surroundings. Although still somewhat dazed, there was growing in him a resentful realization that the rat-faced Tirio was responsible for his present predicament.

The room was about twenty feet square. On two sides were window openings, through which he could see blue sky and white clouds. He limped over to one of the windows and looked out and down. The room where he stood was in the second story of a stone castle. Green meadows stretched away to a wide river. Beyond the river were more fields, and then woods. Just this side of the woods a herd of large, stocky, russet-colored animals was browsing; but they were too far away for Mayhew to make out what they were.

He turned to the other window. Nothing there but rolling meadows, with blue hills beyond.

He turned back to the room. It was bare of all furnishings.

One of the walls held a massive wooden door. In the fourth wall there was a small arched opening into another room, similar to the one he was in.

In fact, so exactly alike were the two rooms, perhaps this supposed opening was merely a mirror. Mayhew stepped over to investigate; sure enough, a replica of himself approached him from the other side.

Mayhew paused and surveyed his image. Not so battered up as he had thought! He grinned. His image grinned back at him.

Then he noticed that the reflection wore a striped toga, whereas he had thought that his toga was gone. He glanced down at himself; he had nothing on but his underwear, dirty and bedraggled underwear at that. He glanced back at the mirror, with a puzzled expression on his face; but the face in the mirror continued to grin.

Then the man in the mirror spoke.

"So it's true," said the man, and stepped through the opening towards him.

CHAPTER VI

"PORTO"

AS THE IMAGE of himself stepped out of the mirror and confronted him, Adams Mayhew fell back a pace, and gasped with astonishment.

"Who—who are you?" he asked.

The reply astonished him even more. It was a single word: "Porto!"

That strange word again! But here at last was the chance to solve the mystery of its meaning.

"What does that mean?" asked Mayhew.

"What does what mean?" countered the other man.

"That word. That awful word 'porto'!"

"Awful?" laughed the man. " 'Porto' isn't a *word*, it's my name. I'm Porto. Do you mean to say that you've been doubling for me all these weeks and have never heard my name?"

It was now Mayhew's turn to laugh.

"I've heard it often enough," he said, "but I never knew what it meant. I thought that it was some sort of insulting epithet, and so I always felt reluctant to inquire about it. If I had inquired the explanation would probably have solved a lot of questions which have been puzzling me."

"For instance?"

"Well, Tirio's hatred for me, and Eleria's scorn."

The face of his double clouded.

"So Eleria is scornful, is she?" he asked. "Curse of Ra! Then

43

she believes me a coward! I credited her with more trustfulness than that."

"But who are you, and what is this all about?" Mayhew inquired.

"I must be brief," Porto replied, glancing nervously around, "for we haven't very much time. I'll give you only the high spots of my story. Tirio hates me—never mind why—partly because of a girl, and partly because he fears my interference in certain schemes in which he has secretly engaged. So he publicly challenged me to a blood feud, although he knows that I am more than a match for him."

"That was either courageous or rash of him."

"It was neither. For, instead of facing me personally, he caused me to be shanghaied aboard a trading vessel, and then gave out the story that I had run away for fear of him. But," bitterly, "I never expected Eleria to believe any such yarn about me. Well, anyway, I escaped from the ship one night, swam to another ship, and eventually landed in disguise at a small port on this island. Imagine my surprise at learning that I had already returned several weeks before, and had had a fight with Tirio on the wharves, but since then had remained in hiding in the house of Julo, afraid to meet Tirio again."

"But, what are you doing *here?*"

"Early last evening, on arriving at the city, still disguised, I learned that Tirio had just kidnaped me, and had disappeared with me. Knowing his habits, and his hangouts, I came directly here with quite a crowd of choice friends, whom I had hurriedly gathered, though I had some difficulty—thanks to you—to persuade them that I hadn't turned coward."

Mayhew began to protest, but his double silenced him with, "I'm sorry I was rude, but you can readily understand how I feel. This castle is now surrounded, but of course my friends won't interfere, so long as Tirio fights fairly and doesn't call in any of his thugs."

"Tell me one more thing," asked Mayhew. "Is Tirio allied with the Spider?"

Porto looked startled, then thoughtful.

"He might be, at that," he said judiciously. "I wouldn't put it beyond him, if he had a chance, for he, too, has been plotting against the government. Of course, no one knows who belongs to that sinister organization. And yet I rather think that Tirio does not. One of his own best friends was recently marked for slaughter."

"All the more reason to suspect him, if you'd ask me."

BUT PORTO interrupted with, "Now you and I must hurry and exchange clothes. I'm fully armed. I want that rat-faced Tirio to get the surprise of his life when he comes here to badger you, or me, or whichever of us he thinks you are."

Mayhew laughed. Then asked, "How did you get in? And how am I to get out?"

"I climbed up a vine on one of the towers, and then, by means of a rope, I crawled down to one of the windows of the next room. I'll get the rope now."

He stepped out through the archway and in a moment was back with the rope, saying, "With this I can lower you down to the ground."

"But I don't like the idea of sneaking out of here," objected Mayhew. "Wouldn't it be much more fun for the two of us to confront Tirio together? Let's one of us fight him and pretend to get knocked out by him, and then have the other one of us step into the room and carry on. He'll think he is seeing a ghost."

Porto smiled appreciatively, but shook his head.

"It would never do!" he asserted. "This is a blood feud, so I must vanquish him alone and unaided. Come on, change clothes with me, and let me lower you out the window; the guards will be here any moment with your breakfast."

But just then there came the sound of the sliding back of the bar which held the door.

Suddenly the waters sank down, sickenly, sucking
Mayhew and the body he was holding, with him

"Too late!" whispered Porto. "All right, we'll have to try your scheme. Sit down and look weak and dazed. I'll step into the next room and await developments."

As they both did as planned, the door swung open, and Tirio entered, clad in the tunic of the police. Striding truculently over to where Mayhew lay on the floor, Tirio addressed him, "Well, fellow, do you still claim that you are not Porto?"

"Oh, no," replied Mayhew readily enough. "I'm willing to admit that I'm any one you say I am."

"Good!" exulted Tirio, rubbing his hands together. "I guess that the manhandling my men gave you last night knocked some of the cockiness out of you. Come, stand up and let me take a look at you."

"I don't choose to get up," said Mayhew simply, continuing to lie on the floor.

Tirio's face went red.

"Don't you realize that you are alone in my castle, and at my mercy!" he shouted.

"Am I alone?" asked Mayhew innocently. "Now, you know, I thought that there were at least two of me here."

"Enough of this foolishness!" exclaimed Tirio, drawing his broadsword from its scabbard at his waist and waving it menacingly. "Stand up or, by Ra, I'll cut a hole in you."

Mayhew scrambled hastily to his feet.

"I'm sure you wouldn't do anything like that," he said in a mock ingratiating manner. "You are by far too honorable a centurion to violate the rules of blood-feudery. I am unarmed, as you have doubtless noticed; so it wouldn't be exactly ethical, would it, for you to cut a hole in me, as you so naively suggest?"

But Tirio had by now sufficiently recovered his composure so as not to be irritated by this line of sarcasm. Instead of flaring up again, he met sneer with sneer, and coolly announced, "You think so? Well, you will never carry back to the city any word of my chivalry; and there is no one else here to note whether or not I observe all the exact niceties of the blood-feud code."

"Isn't there, though?" said a quiet voice behind the centurion.

TIRIO WHEELED to confront a man standing in the archway to the adjoining room, a man toga-clad and calm, with arms folded. Quite a different person from the dirty, disheveled, toga-less man whom he had just been baiting; and yet strangely the same.

"Porto!" exclaimed Tirio aghast.

"The same," replied the vision. Then, whipping out his sword, "Prepare to defend yourself."

"But who—?"

"Oh, just my double. There's two of me, you know."

"But it's against the rules!" Tirio fairly screamed. "You're taking a mean advantage of me!"

"Just as you took unfair advantage of Adamo Mayho here?"

taunted Porto. "Oh, no. I'll do my own fighting, and Mayho will keep out of it."

At the mention of this name, the centurion steadied somewhat.

"So he isn't you, then?" he exclaimed with a relieved gasp.

"Naturally not!" Porto scornfully replied. "I have no occult power, whereby to duplicate or project myself. Come on and fight."

"But how can I know that he will keep out of the fight?"

"In the first place, he is unarmed. In the second place, you have my word of honor. In the third place, you have *his*. Hasn't he, Mayho?"

"Yes," replied Mayhew, "that is as long as he plays fair."

"I doubt it," said Tirio. "Help!" he suddenly shouted.

"Quick, Mayho, the door!"

Steps were heard running toward them in the corridor, and shouts of, "Yes, captain, we come."

The door was standing open, toward them. The stout wooden bar which sometimes served to lock it from the outside was leaning against the door-casing.

Porto glanced around at the opening and quick as a flash the centurion lunged at him with his sword. But Porto turned in time and deflected the blow with his toga-wrapped left arm, then lunged back at his opponent. Tirio, being clad in a tunic rather than in a toga, parried the blow with his sword; but was forced to fall back away from the door.

Meanwhile Mayhew leaped past the two contending men, snatched up the bar, slammed the door shut, and wedged the bar slantwise against it, with the bottom of the bar in a crack between two of the stones of the floor.

And just in time! For several heavy bodies immediately crashed against the portal from the outside. Mayhew threw his weight downward upon the bar, thus wedging it more tightly in place, then turned to watch the fighting.

Mayhew's double was driving the centurion slowly backward around the room; and, even as Mayhew looked, dealt the man a cut across the left shoulder, and then recoiled just enough to avoid a vicious swipe in return.

Tirio felt gingerly of his wound with his left hand, and shouted, "Help!"

"Enough of that!" crisply admonished Porto. "There's a well-armed force of my friends concealed in the tall grass just outside this castle, a force strong enough to be more than a match for all your henchmen. I've a whistle here. If you try any trickery, or if your thugs succeed in breaking down that door, I shall blow the whistle, and you'll never live to tell that you defeated me."

But Tirio continued to call for help. The thudding of shoulders against the door changed to sharp blows as of a battering ram. The door quivered and shook at each impact, but the wedged bar held.

PORTO CONTINUED to drive Tirio backward around the room. Again his blade flashed out, nicking the centurion's arm. Porto's face wore a grim smile. He had established his supremacy over his enemy and was now playing with him.

But suddenly Tirio's yells for help ceased. A sly look of cunning crept into his evil face and his eyes narrowed dangerously as he edged toward a certain portion of the wall of the room. The pounding on the door increased in violence.

At last Tirio threw up his hands and stumbled backward. Porto lunged forward at him, sword extended at full arm's length. The stroke almost reached the unprotected breast of its intended victim. But the rat-faced Tirio had gauged exactly his own backward leap.

And now, as Porto recovered from his lunge, Tirio, instead of sweeping in on him, stepped sidewise and flung his weight against one of the stones of the wall. The stone yielded slightly, and at the same instant the section of floor on which Porto was standing gave way and Porto dropped into a yawning black abyss.

A stifled scream of surprise. The clatter of a sword on a metal chute. The swish of a sliding body. A dull thud. Then silence.

Tirio straightened and turned, broadsword in hand, to face the unarmed Adams Mayhew.

"Your turn next, Mayho," he growled.

For a moment the young American stood dazed by this sudden turn of events.

Then he cringed backward in apparent fear against the wall. The centurion, his evil little eyes, snapping hate, strode over toward him, sword aloft.

But Mayhew's terror had been only pretended. His apparent cringe was really a crouch. As the sword was about to sweep down upon his unarmed form, he suddenly launched himself catlike upon his adversary. His left hand caught the sword-wrist of the centurion. The fingers of his right hand seized the other's throat. His face he buried in the other's breast, to shield it from the blows which Tirio's left hand now showered upon Mayhew's head.

For a moment they swayed together thus, then crashed down in a heap upon the stone flagging, close by the edge of the yawning hole through which Porto had disappeared.

The pounding on the door continued.

Mayhew dug the fingers of his left hand into his adversary's wrist until the sword dropped and went clattering down the chute. Then he transferred this hand, too, to Tirio's throat and squeezed mightily, oblivious of the blows now rained upon him by both fists of the latter.

The centurion's eyes bulged. His face became purple. His lips were flecked with foam. His blows gradually weakened. Then his entire body went limp.

At the same instant one upper corner of the door gave way with a crash.

THERE WAS no time to lose. If Mayhew would save his friend and double, Porto, he must get out of here before the minions of his enemy got in. Heaving the body down the chute, to the accompaniment of shouts of baffled rage from the faces which showed through the splintered aperture of the door, he leaped across to one of the windows, and shouted, "Help! Help for Porto!"

The tall grass waved below in the morning sunlight, but nothing else happened. There was no sign of the friends of Porto.

A knife, hurled through the hole in the door, struck the side of the window casing, glanced off, and dropped to the ground below. The men at the door of the room were now rapidly enlarging the opening with axes.

Seizing Porto's rope which lay in a heap on the floor, Mayhew tied one end to an iron hook which projected from the wall beside the window, threw the other end out, and lowered himself over the edge. A sword whizzed by his head. His last view of the room, as his face disappeared below the sill, disclosed one of the thugs of Tirio clambering through the now enlarged hole in the door.

Down the rope scuttled the young American. The rope parted above him, tumbling him to the ground in a heap. A sword dropped point-down beside him, missing him by a fraction of an inch. Then he quickly regained his feet and stumbled off through the tall grass toward the grove of trees which was supposed to conceal the friends of Porto.

Once he glanced back, and saw the window which he had quitted, framing a half-dozen evil men in blue-bordered tunics, shaking their fists and shouting maledictions after him.

The grass of the meadow was waist high. As Mayhew was striding along through it a man suddenly rose from its concealment, and confronted him with the question, "Where are you going, Porto?"

Was this friend, or foe?

"Who are you?" asked Adams Mayhew, at once on the alert.

The man sneered.

"You've been acting very queerly of late, Porto," he said. "But can it be that you have forgotten your friend Angosto?"

"I'm *not* Porto," Mayhew replied. "I'm merely his double, and the reason for all these seemingly queer actions of your friend is that I haven't known until just now that he and I were twins."

"A likely story, Porto."

"But I'm *not* Porto," Mayhew excitedly exclaimed. "Quick! Porto is in trouble. He was winning the blood-feud, when Tirio suddenly opened a chute in the floor, and Porto disappeared. Where are his friends? We must hurry back and rescue him!"

"Hold on," objected Angosto. "You are Porto yourself. You've been defeated by Tirio. He has stripped your clothes from you. And you are now running away. You look pretty much of a wreck, if you'd ask me."

"I didn't ask you," exclaimed Mayhew, beginning to lose his temper. "But we are wasting valuable time. Porto is in danger."

A third man stood up out of the surrounding grass and joined them.

"What's all the dispute about?" he asked.

"Porto is afraid to fight Tirio, and is sneaking home," sneered Angosto.

WHIRLING AROUND to face the new-comer, Mayhew exclaimed, "You look as though you had brains. Will you take a chance that I'm telling the truth when I say that I'm not Porto, and that Porto is in danger due to Tirio's trickery?"

"Who are you, then?" asked the other, incredulously.

Chafing at the delay, Mayhew briefly recounted his adventures since landing on Mu. But as to his origin, he merely said that he came from a small settlement on the continent that had no name, and that his boat had been sunk off the shores of Mu. Not even to the kindly Julo had he ever related the true details of his fall overboard and the disappearance of the whaling barque Alaska; for these were too incredible.

When Mayhew had completed his story the newcomer determinedly announced, "I'll take the chance. We'll attack the castle at once. And, if it turns out that you really are Porto after all, as even I still believe, we can turn you over to Tirio and wash our hands of you."

"Fair enough," agreed Mayhew. "Come on."

The man pulled a whistle from the folds of his toga, and blew it. Instantly a dozen men arose from the grass on all sides and came hurrying over. The situation was explained in a few words to their incredulous ears; and then, drawing their swords with a resolute cheer, they set out for the castle.

During the latter part of the conversation Mayhew had been vaguely conscious of a loud and distant droning noise, like a woodpecker pounding on a tin roof. Now, as they started toward the castle of Tirio, Mayhew glanced around in an attempt to locate the source of this peculiar sound. It came from overhead. Far aloft, sweeping toward them, was what looked like a huge dragonfly, with rigid tail and four wings projecting sideward from near its head. The noise, reverberating against the flawless blue of the sky, became almost deafening as the thing approached. All the party stared up at it.

"What's that?" gasped Mayhew.

"Don't you know, Porto?" asked Angosto, incredulously. "Oh, I forgot, you claim not to be Porto. That thing is one of the flying chariots of the priesthood of Ra."

"A flying machine?" gasped Mayhew. "Some crazy scientists in my own country have claimed that men will sometime learn to fly, but of course that's absurd."

"The priesthood have been doing it here for years," Angosto explained, "but no one knows how they do it. It's a closely guarded secret, and the weird things are seldom seen."

The airplane passed by and out of sight. By this time Mayhew and Angosto and the other friends of Porto had reached the door of Tirio's castle.

"Now how are we to get in?" asked one.

To their surprise the door was flung open and one of the tunic-clad thugs rushed out.

"A truce!" he called. "A truce! The castle is overrun with spider-men! Come help us against the common enemy."

"Death to the spider-men!" shouted the leader of Mayhew's party. "Come on! But," he urged in a lower tone of voice, "beware of treachery."

Then, with drawn swords, they charged through the open doorway into the dark interior of Tirio's castle.

CHAPTER VII

THE SPIDER-MEN

THEY EYES OF the invaders had scarcely adapted themselves to the dimness of this lower corridor of Tirio's castle, after
the contrasting bright tropical sunlight outside when they were
set upon by a veritable pack of little yellow men.

Mayhew stumbled over a prostrate body and fell to his hands
and knees. He could see more distinctly now. The body wore a
blue and white tunic. The fighting passed on into the interior.

A sword was clutched in the dead fingers. Mayhew freed it
and weighed it in his own hand. Then an idea came to him: if
he was to rescue Porto, how better than by disguising himself as
one of the forces of Tirio? So he hastily donned the tunic and
armlets of the fallen thug. Then he too pressed on toward the
noise of the fighting.

Another tunic-clad individual entered from a side corridor.
Before this man was aware of Mayhew's presence, Mayhew had
seized the man's shoulder and had pressed the point of his blade
against the man's ribs.

"Lead me to the dungeon at the foot of the chute, which runs
from the tower room," he hissed.

"Who are you?" asked the man, squirming a bit.

"Never mind," Mayhew replied. "Lead on. And no treachery."

"But we are all friends for the moment," objected the thug.
"The castle is overrun with spider-men."

"How do you know?" asked the American. "I thought that no
one had ever seen a spider-man."

"No one ever has before today. But these are spider-men, all right. Look!"

Mayhew looked. In the hallway in front of them stood two small, slant-eyed, Oriental-looking individuals, each holding a pair of sharp daggers. Each was clad in a flaming red tunic, on the breast and back of which was emblazoned the black, squat, repulsive spider symbol, with which Mayhew had become so familiar. A moment ago the corridor had been empty.

As he stared at these two weird new-comers, they sprang. One launched himself at Mayhew, the other at Mayhew's captive. The American swung his blade at the left wrist of his assailant, at the same time crouching and driving his left fist into the man's midriff. The man crumpled, and Mayhew dropped astride him and disarmed him.

Glancing up, the American satisfied himself that his companion was holding his own in the knife duel with the other spider-man; then turned his attention back to the man beneath him. But, to his surprise, he found himself, kneeling astride of nothing! The spider-man was no longer there. And yet Mayhew had not felt him wriggle out from under.

Passing his left hand perplexedly through his sandy hair, Mayhew scrambled to his feet and looked hastily and alertly around. But he stood alone in the corridor. The two spider-men and the minion of Tirio had all vanished into thin air!

HE SHOOK his head with perplexity, and much disturbed, passed cautiously on along the corridor. A stairway attracted his attention and gave him an idea. If he could get to the tower room in which he and Porto had fought with Tirio, perhaps he could go down the chute and find his friend. He sped up the stairs.

In the upper hall he found a coil of rope. The room which he sought, he identified by its broken door. Yes, there was the hole in the floor, still gaping open.

He knelt at its edge and stared down, but could see nothing except the beginning of the chute, shading off into the black depths below.

"Porto!" he called. "Tirio!"

No answer.

So, sheathing his sword, he tied his rope to the hook by the window, and then threw its other end down the chute.

But, just as he knelt to lower himself down the chute, he was pounced upon from all sides by a perfect swarm of little yellow spider-men. The attack was unexpected. He had not heard or seen them enter the room. Yet here they were, and he was unarmed and at their mercy.

Against overwhelming odds he fought. Fought, though he lay upon the floor beneath a pile of humanity. He heard one of the enemy gasp and then go shrieking down the chute, to a thud and silence.

His own wind was cut off. He strained to breathe.

Gradually Adams Mayhew's senses cleared again. He still lay at the bottom of a pile of warm and smelly human bodies, but they were picking themselves up. He drew great gulps of air into his tortured lungs, but the air tasted sulphurous and strangely unrefreshing. Although the mist cleared from his eyes, the redness of all his surroundings still persisted.

He struggled to his feet and stared around, but recognized nothing.

Although he had not passed completely out—he was sure of that one fact—nevertheless the room of Tirio's castle, where he had been but an instant before, had now miraculously metamorphosed into a vaulted cave with stalactite-covered walls and ceiling, lit by the reddish glare of flickering torches.

On the ground beside him lay another man, the henchman of Tirio, by whose side he had fought in the lower hallway of the castle, and who had so miraculously disappeared in the midst of that fight. Around the two of them stood scores of the little yellow men, in their red tunics with the spider insigne.

One of them was announcing, "Excellency, we bring you the last two of the wearers of the blue and white."

"Fools!" hissed a voice, and its metallic menace sent a chill through Mayhew and caused the hairs to rise on the back of his neck. "Fools, this is not the man. Neither of these is the centurion Tirio."

Mayhew's gaze sought the source of this obscene voice.

He saw a square-cut throne of blood-red marble. On each of the two corners of the top of the back there reposed a white and grinning human skull. In the seat of this throne there sprawled a black spider with a yellow face! Was it a spider? Or was it a man?

Yes, it was a man. But what a creature! It was a fat, squat, bloated hunchback, clad in a tight-fitting, closely-knitted black garment. Lean clawlike fingers gripped the two arms of the throne.

THE CREATURE'S head was bald and parchment-skinned. Its eyes were slanted. Its nose and chin were both hooked, until they nearly met. Its mouth was wide, its lips thin and cruel; and through them there projected two long, sharp, white dog-teeth, like poison fangs.

"Take them away," it croaked, waving one taloned hand toward Mayhew and his prostrate companion. "Take them away and feed them to the eternal fires."

Instantly several of the little yellow men leaped upon Mayhew and tied his arms behind his back before he had a chance to resist. The henchman of Tirio was jerked to his feet and similarly tied. Then the two of them were prodded with sharp knives out of the presence of the repulsive creature on the red marble throne.

To the accompaniment of many flaming torches they were driven through winding passageways of solid rock. It seemed they went miles. It became a treadmill existence like sleepwalking. When either of them stumbled and fell, as occurred increasingly often, the luckless one was kicked and prodded and knifed to his feet again.

Gradually the smell of sulphur in the air became more and more oppressive. A flickering red glare, somehow different from that of the torches, loomed ahead down the corridor. At regular intervals a shriek of agony could be heard. Each shriek ended abruptly, as though suddenly snuffed out.

Finally the passageway widened out into a huge cave, at the far end of which there was an inferno of flames, rising from the level of the floor and extending a hundred feet or more upward, to disappear through an aperture in the roof. Silhouetted against these fires were four or five small groups of men, and at the very edge of the flaming abyss there stood a score or more individuals armed with long spears.

As Mayhew's party entered the chamber, one of the groups ahead bustled a resisting figure up into the midst of the spearmen, who promptly presented the points of their spears to the poor creature's back and forced him to the brink. He struggled to escape them, but he had to move or be impaled, until at last he toppled over the edge with a despairing shriek which came to an abrupt end with a puff of flame.

It reminded Adams Mayhew of a moth flying into a lamp, and being suddenly snuffed out.

Victim after victim was driven over the edge of the eternal flames, until finally there were left only Mayhew and the henchman of Tirio. Of these two, Mayhew's turn came first. In spite of his struggles, he was prodded forward and turned over to the spearmen. His bonds were cut, doubtless to render his death agonies more interesting. Then, with the sharp spears pricking into his back, the relentless march to the flaming brink began.

He reached the edge and looked down. And now he saw that what he had taken for flames, when viewed from the entrance to the cavern, was not flames at all, but rather the reflections from a seething caldron below, cast upon a rising cloud of smoke and steam. He glanced upward, and saw this cloud being sucked into an unending funnel above, a veritable chimney.

DOWN AGAIN into the pit he stared. Not more than twenty or thirty feet below the ledge on which he stood, there boiled and surged a lake of molten fire. It flowed and seethed and jostled. Parts of it bubbled upward, and then spread outward like springs of glowing water. Still other parts, caught between two opposite streams, eddied and whirled.

Sometimes real flames would leap upward and lap the rock on which he stood. One such flame, reaching higher than the others, singed his hair and eyebrows and eyelashes, and drove him back against the sharp points of spears.

Recoiling from a score of cuts, he leaned suddenly forward again, lost his balance, and toppled at the brink. But, with a mighty effort, he flung his body back against the spear-points, and did not flinch as they bit into his flesh again.

The rock upon which he stood crumbled. His sandaled feet slid over the edge, and he landed sitting on the very brink. The smell of burning flesh—or leather—assailed his nostrils, and intense pain shot through his legs.

Flinging himself upon his back, he lifted his legs high out of the licking flames, only to have them beaten down again with the points of spears. Other spear-points jabbed into his neck and shoulders, and pushed him slowly toward the edge.

With one last despairing effort, he rolled over onto his face. His entire body from the waist down was now hanging over the flames, but the caldron was for the instant indulging in one of its momentary lulls, and the cool breeze, which the draft of the devil's chimney sucked through the caverns toward this spot, reduced to some extent the searing heat on his lower limbs.

He grabbed for the haft of one of the prodding spears, only to have the sharp edges of its point tear his palm as it was yanked from his grasp. Again he grabbed, this time with both hands and higher up. And this time he was prepared for the backward yank. He held tight, and threw up one knee.

Out of the pit he came. And when the spearman, too late, changed his tactics and thrust instead of pulling, Mayhew was already on his feet again, and able to push the spear to one side and let go.

Then, before the spearman could recover or any of the others could jab, Mayhew lunged forward, flung his arms around the spearman, dragged him to the floor, and rolled over with the spearman on top, so that the latter's body would protect him momentarily at least, from the thrusts of the others.

In this position, the American held on like grim death.

For a few seconds Mayhew was able to hold the body of the spearman protectingly above him. But knives, jabbing into the muscles of his arms, soon loosened his hold, and the man was dragged off of him.

Mayhew was jerked to his feet and, bleeding and staggering, was once more hustled to the edge of the pit.

As he tottered at the brink, a shout of command echoed through the chamber. The spear-thrusts ceased; but Mayhew, too weak to stand any longer, lurched over the edge into the eternal flames.

CHAPTER VIII

TO BE A SLAVE

THE NEXT THING Mayhew knew he was lying painfully on a hard stone floor, while a group of men, weirdly illumined by flickering red light, were standing above him, arguing about something.

"But I tell you the boss said he wanted two, not one."

"Maybe so. Maybe so. But what good is this fellow, thoroughly scorched and full of spear-holes?"

"There's no harm in trying him. If he lives and stands the work, well and good. If he dies, he dies. And if he lives and can't do the work, back he can go to, the eternal fires."

At this point Mayhew interposed with a faint, "What happened? Didn't I fall into the volcano?"

"You did, fellow," one of the guards replied. "But I dropped my spear, reached over, and grabbed you, just in the nick of time. You nearly pulled me in with you. And now, after all my trouble, some of these yellow friends of mine insist on throwing you back in again."

The speaker, although he wore the red tunic of the forces of the spider, had the features of a white man.

"But I don't understand," persisted Mayhew, now sitting up and staring around him. "Why was I pulled out at all?"

"Somebody yelled, 'Stop! Save him! We need two!'" explained the white spearman. "And so, without thinking, I grabbed."

"Two what?" asked Mayhew.

"Two slaves. His excellency, the spider, keeps a certain number of thousands of slaves. All over that number go to feed the fires of our goddess."

"Then you don't worship Ra?"

"Pele forbid!" chanted the group in unison.

Things were going fine. So long as Mayhew could keep up this conversation, he was staving off the fatal trip back to the eternal fires. He brightened perceptibly, in spite of the pain of his burns, and his faintness from loss of blood.

"So I'm to be a slave?" he mused aloud.

"Not a chance," replied one of the group. "You're too done for."

"Look here," said the white spearman, wheeling around upon the last speaker. "The boss sent for two, didn't he? Well, then, we'll send him two." Then to Mayhew, "Stand up, fellow. If you can make it, your life is saved. Good luck to you."

The American staggered to his feet. His tunic was gone—burned off, probably. His sandals were charred. His legs were blistered. One hand was throbbing painfully. And he was covered with blood.

But he was still alive!

"Lead on," said he, grimly setting his teeth.

"Just a minute," interposed the white spearman.

Walking over to Mayhew, he placed, one of his feet alongside one of the American's and studied the comparison.

"A bit large," he mused, "but all the better. Here, fellow, sit down while I fix you up."

Mayhew was glad enough to obey.

But one of the yellow spearmen objected.

"You're a sentimental fool," he said.

The white spearman wheeled around upon him with a menacing, "Pele is hungry for such as you."

The objector promptly subsided. Then the white spearman reached up under his own red tunic and removed his nether undergarment, which he tore into strips. Tenderly unfastening the charred remains of Mayhew's sandals, he bound these strips around his feet. Then he removed his own sandals and adjusted them over these bandages.

"There, fellow," he said, getting to his feet and dusting off his hands, "now you have a fighting chance to survive."

Mayhew, too, arose.

"Thank you ever so much—" he began.

But his benefactor cut him off with, "It's nothing. I may be an exile from my own people, but I'm still human."

"His excellency shall hear of this," muttered one of the others.

"And if so, so will Pele," snapped the white spearman.

"Let's get going," interrupted the messenger who had come for the two slaves. "And I'll need two guards."

"Take Tolofo. We don't want him," chorused several.

AND SO it was that Tolofo, the white spearman who had befriended Mayhew, was one of those to accompany him on his long and painful pilgrimage.

The two prisoners and the messenger carried torches. Tolofo and the other guard carried spears. In addition, the messenger and the two guards wore broadswords hung from a belt of polished steel links.

The route led for about a mile through winding subterranean tunnels. Mayhew gritted his teeth and struggled to keep up with the others, but it was grim work.

Finally they reached the foot of a circular shaft, through the far distant top of which could be seen the blue sky. Around the walls of this shaft there ran a spiral staircase, up which the party began to climb.

Mayhew's feet by now had ceased to hurt. But, what was worse, they had become numb. He had hard work controlling them; they refused to track, yet he stumbled upward.

In his unsteady condition, fearing the sheer edge of the steps, unguarded by any rail, he hugged the wall, until the yellow spearman, bringing up the rear, bumped against him. Unable to recover his balance, he lurched toward the edge. The yellow spearman jabbed at him with his weapon; but Tolofo, turning, drove in with his own spear, warding off the blow, and with the same motion forcing Mayhew back upon the step.

"It would be very unfortunate," Tolofo remarked in a casual tone, "if a yellow spearman should accidentally fall to the bottom of this shaft."

"It would be more unfortunate," interposed the messenger, "if some one were to report how it happened."

"And it would be still more unfortunate," the white spearman retorted, "if two yellow men fell down the shaft."

The party resumed their upward climb, Tolofo keeping close to Mayhew, and between him and the edge, the rest of the way up.

At last they reached the top, and stood on a mountain spur. Behind them towered the smoking volcano, which Mayhew had seen before, but never so close as this. Before them were foothills, and beyond those were rolling prairies beribboned with streams, and dotted with groves, villages and farms. In the far dim distance shone the domes and minarets of the Golden City, and beyond that sparkled the sea.

The clear mountain air felt most refreshing after the sulphurous fumes and the torch-smoke of the caverns. The light of Ra, the sun, was most cheering, after the red glare of Pele, the fire goddess.

Mayhew's head began to clear. His wounds had already limbered up considerably, and now the feeling began to return to his numbed legs.

For a few moments the party sat on the rocks and rested, then they turned to the left and took up a winding trail along a shoulder of the mountain. For hour after hour they trudged on, over rough volcanic rocks, sometimes uphill, sometimes down, but rarely on the level.

TO KEEP his mind off his troubles, Mayhew let his thoughts dwell on the crowded affairs of the last few hours. Less than a day ago he had been peacefully living in the Golden City of Mu, a guest of the magistrate Julo. Since then he had been kidnaped by Tirio; had met his own double, Porto; had fought first against the forces of Tirio, and then with them against the spider-men; had been miraculously spirited away from Tirio's castle to the caves of living fire, where he had met the spider face to face; had been almost sacrificed to Pele; and finally had trudged miles and miles.

He thought of Eleria. Mistaking Adams Mayhew for his double, Porto, and misinterpreting his ignorance for cowardice, she had never relented, had never unbent toward him. And yet it was her presence in the Golden City, and the hope of breaking down her reserve and eventually making her acquaintance, that had reconciled Adams Mayhew to the gradually growing realization that for him at least, America somehow no longer existed, and that he was doomed to spend the rest of his existence on the continent of Mu.

With these thoughts he plodded doggedly on. His thought became blurred and incoherent. On a treadmill, through a thick haze, he pursued the floating vision of a cameo-cut face, surmounted by an aureole of honey-colored hair. At length, even this face vanished. A black fog engulfed him. Adams Mayhew was "out on his feet."

"Halt!" sung out a peremptory voice ahead of them. "Who comes?"

The five men halted. Mayhew swayed for a moment. Then his knees crumpled, and he sunk silently to the ground.

Ages later, he came to his senses again. Every muscle of his body ached. His feet and legs stung and throbbed excruciatingly. But he was lying on soft mats, and over him was bending a kindly face masked behind a luxuriant and bushy blond beard.

"Well, fellow," said the voice of Tolofo, "you've had a long, hard pull, but you've made it."

"Where am I?" weakly asked the American.

"At one of the labor camps of his excellency."

"And what are *you* doing here?"

"I've had a stroke of luck, which shows that it pays to do a kind deed. When we reached here ten days ago, one of the foremen had just died. The boss liked my looks and gave me the job. So here I am, sitting pretty. All of which is probably a good thing for you, too. I had quite an argument with the boss as to what to do with you."

"I suppose he wanted to send me back to Pele," wryly.

"Not at all. Much simpler than that. Just heave you into the sea."

"Are we near the sea?" asked Mayhew, an immense longing welling into his heart.

"Just a few hundred paces."

Mayhew sat up and sniffed the salt breeze. In the not far distance he could hear the pounding of surf upon rocks, and the sucking rattle of pebbles under receding waves. A smile formed upon his face and he sank back contentedly among the sleeping mats.

"You'll do, fellow," remarked Tolofo approvingly.

CHAPTER IX

THE STORM

A FEW DAYS later Mayhew was up and about. He had been staying in the foreman's own private cave, but now he was transferred to one of the prison cells of the workers, an evil smelling hole, barred with an iron grating and shared by a dozen rough men.

This entire squad, which Tolofo commanded, was made up of white men. Some had been gentlemen before their capture by the Spider, and some had been bums, but all were now indistinguishably vicious and desperate.

Tolofo ruled them with an iron hand, yet always with such fairness and consideration that the men soon grew to respect and almost love him. A warm bond sprang up between him and Mayhew. At first the other men resented this, but after Mayhew had thrashed the camp bully for accusing Tolofo of favoritism, they respected him too.

This particular labor camp was located near the head of a deep rocky fjord. Inland from the fjord and separated from it by a thin but high wall of rock was a small salt-water lake, in which the tide rose and fell in unison with the sea outside, thus indicating some concealed connection between the two. From this lake, the slaves of the Spider were employed in tunneling into the heart of the mountain, for the rumored purpose of providing a canal, which should lead to a secret harbor, close and convenient to the throne-room of his excellency.

Other labor battalions were at work excavating this supposed harbor, and in digging outward therefrom to meet the tunnel on which Mayhew and his fellow laborers were engaged.

Mayhew's wounds and burns at last were healed. His singed hair grew out again, long and unkempt. And a bushy blond beard developed. Soon he was able to do a day's digging alongside the best of them.

Then came the day of the great storm. The gang was working in the tunnel, when the sea end of it gave way to the beating of the waves, and a sudden rush of waters engulfed them. An instant ago they had been picking and shoveling, by the light of a score of flares. Now they found themselves caught and tumbled about in the swirl of a whirlpool, with all of the torches but one extinguished. Toward that one light they fought, choking, gasping, clawing at each other and at every projection of rock.

MAYHEW WAS the first to reach firm ground and drag himself out upon a ledge.

Above the reverberating din of the pounding waves, he shouted, "Use your heads! Help each other! Don't fight!"

Another slave pulled himself up on the ledge beside the American and lay whimpering. Mayhew shook him into coherence. Then, as successive surges brought the clawing mass of humanity within their reach, they seized two of their friends and pulled them ashore.

Soon all the squad were accounted for. They ceased their efforts and panted from their exertions.

Suddenly one of them exclaimed, "Where's Tolofo?"

All the workers were saved, but not the foreman. Mayhew snatched the torch from its niche, and held it far out over the black waters. Just at the limit of its beams he thought he saw a rising and falling shape which might be a human body.

Handing the flare to the nearest man, he said, "Hold it for me," and plunged in.

He reached the floating shape and grasped it. Just then the light went out. An eddy whirled him around and he lost all sense of direction. Holding tight to the tunic of the body, he

The whirlpool caught them, swirled them

tried to swim toward where he imagined his friends to be; but
suddenly the waters sank down, sickeningly down, down, sucking him with them, and then something hard and sharp struck
his head from above.

For a moment he was stunned, but he never loosened the
grip of his right hand. When he opened his eyes again it was
to the gray daylight of a driving storm. He was in the basin of
the salt lake.

But the return swell was bearing him back again toward the
face of the rock wall of the tunnel. Frantically he attempted to
stem the tide. The waters sucked him on and down. But just as
he reached the face of the cliff the current turned, and carried
him out again. Almost exhausted, he swam toward the rocky
shore of the lake.

Alternately he was swept this way and that, but at last he
made it, and hauled himself and the body of Tolofo out onto
a low pinnacle of rock, where he lay and held on for dear life.

The side of the basin was too steep for him to climb, even if
he had not been burdened by the body of his friend. All he could

do was hold on. The waves broke over him, the storm beat upon him, yet still he held on.

But gradually his hold weakened. He shouted for help, against the roar of wind and wave, but no one answered.

CHAPTER X

ANOTHER IMPERSONATION

ADAMS MAYHEW CLUNG with one hand to the wave washed rock, and with the other to the tunic of Tolofo. He resolved to let go of the rock before he would relinquish his hold on his friend; but he bent every effort to retain both.

A pebble dropped on him. He heard a slipping, scraping sound above the roar of the storm. Glancing up, he saw a man-like shape descending the face of the cliff. A hand reached out and touched him. With a lurch he let go of the rock and grasped the hand. It pulled him to his feet. Then, with the last ounce of strength remaining in him, he passed the body of Tolofo up to the man above.

A few minutes later Mayhew himself was being handed from man to man up the face of the cliff.

The whole squad regathered in the quarters of the foreman. Tolofo at last opened his eyes, but he was very weak, and kept spitting blood.

They told him how Adams Mayhew had rescued him.

"Fellows," said he, "I'm done for. I think my whole side is caved in. Mayho, you're a good fellow. With that beard you look enough like me that a stranger would not know the difference. Why not *be* me? And, when I die, bury Adamo Mayho."

He coughed painfully and spat.

"It hurts to talk," he said, yet he kept on. "You know something of my story; how I fled from the Golden City, an outlaw, accused of a crime of which I was innocent. I have been a spider-man for six moons, a spearman all that time. This—informa-tion—will—enable—you—"

A paroxysm of coughing ensued. His head flopped to one side, and his stiffened body relaxed and slumped. Tolofo, the renegade, was dead.

A subdued gang of burly men stripped the body of its blood red tunic and carried it through wind and rain to the edge of the cliff.

"Too bad we haven't a priest to consign his soul to Pele," mused one.

"To Pele with Pele!" shouted another. "He was white, even if he was a spiderman. His soul will go to Ra."

"I used to work in one of the temples," diffidently put in a third. "I can give part of the ritual."

"Go on," urged a fourth.

So they laid the body face-up upon the rain lashed rocks and the thug who had once been a temple attendant haltingly recited the chant to Ra. As he finished there came a rift in the clouds above and a single beam of sunlight shot down for an instant upon the little funeral group.

"Over with him, while the sun-god smiles!" whispered one, and the body of Tolofo splashed into the raging lake beneath.

"In the name of the Father, and of the Son, and of the Holy Ghost. Amen," said Mayhew under his breath, as he turned away with a tear in his eye.

"Well," remarked one of the others, "we've buried Adamo Mayho. What are your orders, Tolofo?"

Mayhew snapped back to the present.

"My orders," said he quietly, "are that one of you go down to headquarters, report to the boss the breaking of the sea-wall and the drowning of Mayho, and convey my request for an extra issue of wine because of the hardships which you have been through."

"Three cheers for Adamo Mayho!" shouted one.

"Careful!" cautioned another. "You mean: three cheers for Tolofo."

Thus the new Tolofo rose phoenixlike from the ashes of the old.

That night Mayhew slept in the quarters of his friend and former chief, and the next day he took up his duties as foreman of the gang.

At noon a messenger arrived with a letter for Tolofo. Mayhew opened it; then ran his fingers through his hair. The crest of the letter was a squat, sprawled, hairy black spider; that was familiar and understandable enough. But Mayhew had not sufficiently mastered the written language of Mu to be able to make out more than one or two of the hieroglyphics which formed the message.

THIS PRESENTED a quandary. Was Mayhew, in his guise as Tolofo the foreman, supposed to be able to know how to read? Nothing to do but take a chance and find out.

"Any reply?" asked the messenger.

"Speak when you're spoken to," the American curtly answered. "There will be a reply, but I shall not have it ready until tomorrow. Go down to headquarters and ask them to put you up for the night."

When the messenger had departed, Mayhew hastily called his squad together and asked, "In my previous existence did I know how to read?"

No one could remember.

"Can any of you read?"

The man who had worked in a temple claimed to be able to read a little; but, after perusing the letter for several minutes, he had to admit that he could make nothing of it.

Later in the day, the boss came by to see what progress they were making toward clearing up yesterday's debris, and to give them instructions for sinking a new shaft a safe distance back from the present water-filled tunnel. When they had agreed

*As the Oriental girl reached the throne and saw the king
who had summoned her, her face went stark with terror*

upon the details of this new project, Mayhew drew the letter
out of the pouch which hung from his sword belt and handed
it over to the boss.

The latter read it through with pursed lips, then stared fixedly
at Mayhew.

"You've read this yourself, of course?" he asked.

"Well—no," admitted the supposed foreman. "I tried to, but
somehow I couldn't quite catch the drift of it."

"Why, I thought that you could read!" exclaimed the boss.
"You were an educated gentleman before you enlisted under
the Spider."

"True," admitted Mayhew, putting on a sheepish expression.
"But I was a wild youth, and my education was rather neglected.
That's how I came to get into the trouble which drove me to seek
refuge with his excellency."

"Yes, I know," mused the boss. "But you always claimed to
be able to read."

"True again," said Mayhew, "and I threw a pretty good bluff at it, too. I did it in the hope of advancement."

"Well, at least you have the good sense to risk your reputation, rather than to conceal this letter. Are you sure that Adamo Mayho was drowned? That he didn't escape?"

"Why—yes," stammered Mayhew. Then, recovering his poise with an effort, he continued: "Has any one who has gone over the hill ever gotten by the guards?"

"No. But you are reported to have been unduly friendly with this Mayo," pointedly accused the boss.

"He was my best worker," Mayhew boldly countered.

"Well, you have produced wonderful results with your gang," grudgingly admitted the boss. "It's a good thing for Mayho that he *is* dead, if he is; for this letter is an order from his excellency that Mayho be seized and bound at once, as a dangerous character, and sent back to the throne room. Reading between the lines, I think I can see that Pele is hungry."

AT THE close of the work that day Mayhew was still thanking his lucky stars that he had changed places with the dead Tolofo. But he did not remain thankful for long.

As he was locking his squad in their cells for the night, one of them beckoned to him and whispered, "How about leaving the grating unlocked? Some of us might want to go over the hill, you know."

"You're crazy," Mayhew replied. "In the first place, you couldn't make it, even if I helped you. And in the second place, I'm foreman now."

"Is that so?" sneered the other. "What good does it do us to have a fellow slave for foreman, unless he helps us to escape? Think it over for a day or two. One of us overheard you talking with the boss this afternoon, so we know what was in that letter from his excellency, the Spider. We know what is in store for Adamo Mayho, if he gets found out. So think it over—*Tolofo.*"

"I'm doing this for your own good," Mayhew retorted, but somehow his words did not sound particularly convincing.

He did think the matter over—very seriously—that night. Truly he was in a fix, and just when he had thought that everything was rosy. If he helped his former pals to escape, it would mean court-martial for him. And if he did not help them to escape, it would mean exposure and certain death in the eternal fires of Pele.

Late into the night he lay awake, puzzling over his predicament. And at last, along toward morning, a happy solution occurred to him. Perhaps not a happy solution, but at least an alternative which might possibly succeed. He would go over the hill with his men.

If intercepted, his credentials as foreman might possibly get them through, if he could think of a plausible story to explain their presence wherever they happened to be caught. The more he thought of this plan the better it seemed.

At last he arose from his sleeping mats, tiptoed out of his cave, and walked softly to the cave which quartered his men. Tapping on their grating to arouse them and attract their attention, he explained his plan. It was enthusiastically received. He was restored to their good graces.

In fact, as one of them expressed it, "Good old Tolofo is a regular fellow again."

It was decided to make the break the following night. Several of the men knew the surrounding country for quite a distance. But, beyond that, their fate was on the knees of Ra.

But with the morning there came a message summoning him before the boss. And the boss informed him of a decision to send him back to the throne-room of the Spider, to explain to his excellency the strange disappearance of Mayho.

Mayhew's first reaction was intense relief. His problem was solved for him. But the more that he thought about the situation the more he came to realize that he was merely being plunged from one danger into another.

The Spider might see through his assumed identity. Some person at court might recognize him as not being Tolofo. Or his gang, cheated out of their planned escape, might tell the boss that he was an impostor.

Perhaps his men would believe him, when he explained the situation to them. Perhaps they would realize that their own self-interest would be best served by keeping quiet until his return, in the hope that they could then effect the planned escape.

But, when he got back from headquarters to his own cell, he found that a substitute foreman had already led his squad off for the day's work. So, with ominous forebodings, he packed up the few belongings of the predecessor whose name he had assumed and accompanied the messenger of the Spider.

THE RETURN trip was a revelation to Adams Mayhew. Having traversed the road in the reverse direction in a wounded and fainting condition, he had always thought of it as extending interminably for thousands upon thousands of miles. Now, to his intense surprise, he found the trip a remarkably easy one. By noon they had reached the top of the spiral shaft. In a few moments they were at its bottom. And a half hour more brought them to the caves of eternal fire, and the throne room of the Spider.

After a slight wait, Mayhew was ushered into the presence of his excellency. In view of the fact that everything else had appeared to diminish in impressiveness since his first arrival at these mountains, he half expected that the same would hold true of the Spider.

But it did not. The creature squatted, as repulsive and terrifying as ever, on its skull-topped throne of red marble. Again the hair rose involuntarily on the nape of the young man's neck at the awful sight.

At one side of the throne there stood a crystal globe on a steel pedestal. Clutched in his claws, the Spider held a scroll of parchment which he appeared to be perusing.

Mayhew waited until the creature glanced up. Then placing right hand upon left shoulder, according to the Muian custom, he bowed low before the throne.

But the Spider stiffened, and flashed a baleful glance at him, hissing out, "What now, Tolofo, cannot you forget your former nationality?"

Adams Mayhew did some quick thinking. Glancing around, yet without moving his head to indicate that he was doing so, he noted that the two attendants who had led him into the presence of their ruler were both standing erect with right arm extended straight forward, palm to the front.

Instantly he whipped into the same position, stammering, "Your excellency will forgive the fact that your august appearance awed me into a long-accustomed gesture of humility."

The face of the Spider softened into a toothy leer.

"A pretty speech, Tolofo," said he. "But now let us get down to business. I hear that you lost one of your slaves. How did it happen?"

The story which Adams Mayhew then related was one which had been carefully thought up by him on his trek hither across the mountains. It was quite simple, namely a true account of the breaking of the sea-wall, and the subsequent rescue of all the members of the squad except one. But the teller was Tolofo, rather than Adams Mayhew; the missing man was Adamo Mayho, rather than Tolofo; and the story ended right at that point.

"So I led the rest of them back to their cell, sent word to the boss, and drew an extra ration of wine for them. That is all, your excellency."

The Spider fixed him with a piercing stare from beady black eyes. Then lowered his gaze and perused the scroll.

Mayhew shifted his feet uneasily. Had this uncanny creature seen through his deception?

Finally the Spider again looked up at him.

"Tolofo," said he, "something tells me that you are lying to me." He paused to let that sink in; then continued, "And yet your record gives me no cause to suspect you. You are unquestionably a fugitive from the justice of Mu, and thus cannot possibly be conspiring with the empire against me. Since joining my order you have been frank and independent, almost too frank and too independent at times. I know all about your having befriended this Adamo Mayhew; but then there is nothing to indicate that you knew that he was a henchman of the magistrate Julo, who has been plotting my downfall. Julo, the very same judge who convicted you! Had you known that, you would not have befriended Mayho, I feel sure."

"I thank your excellency," murmured Mayhew, inclining his head slightly.

"Don't thank me too quickly," bristled the Spider. Then to the guards, "Take him away, while I meditate on what disposition to make of his case."

CHAPTER XI

THROUGH THE CRYSTAL

ADAMS MAYHEW DID not have long to wait for the decision of the Spider. In a very few minutes he was summoned back into the stalactite encrusted throne room.

This time he made the proper salute, and the squat creature on the throne grinned appreciatively.

"You improve," said he. "How would you like to work for me; Tolofo?"

What new trap was this?

"I do not understand," Mayhew replied guardedly. "Already I have served your excellency faithfully for a matter of six moons."

The Spider bristled.

"Fool!" he hissed. "I mean my personal service."

"The honor overwhelms me."

"You sneer at me!" fairly screamed the Spider, convulsively gripping the arms of the throne with his taloned fingers. Then relaxing, as his mood shifted, he grinned toothily, and said, "But no, I keep forgetting that you are Tolofo, the frank, the truthful. So I believe you."

For the second time that afternoon, Mayhew murmured, "I thank your excellency."

But still he kept his eyes open and his wits alert for some trap.

Again the monarch's mood shifted. Suddenly clapping his hands, "Out of here! Away, all of you. I would speak with Tolofo alone."

The yellow courtiers hurried away. In an instant the cavern was deserted, save for the repulsive creature squatting on the blood-red throne, and the stalwart young American seaman who stood before him.

"And now, Tolofo," said the Spider, "you may sit at my feet."

Lest he irritate the monarch, Mayhew obeyed. The crippled hunchback became almost human. Leaning forward, he gazed down upon the man at his feet with as ingratiating a smile as his twisted features would permit.

"Tell me, Tolofo," he simpered, "am I handsome and awe-inspiring?"

Mayhew played a hunch.

"No, your excellency," he replied with simple directness. "You are never handsome. And for the moment you deign not to be awe-inspiring, although usually you are."

The Spider's hands clenched, and his eyes narrowed. Then he laughed a mirthless cackling laugh.

"You're refreshing," he said. "Oh, these fools, these yellow fools! *They* would have said that I was beautiful. Yet, if I thought myself beautiful, why would I have chosen as my symbol and emblem the repulsive spider which I resemble? And I am glad to learn from your lips that occasionally, when I try, I can cease to be awe-inspiring. Much as I hate your accursed race, I need a *white* man, to tell me the truth. Yes, that shall be your job, Tolofo, to stand at the right hand of the Spider, and tell him the truth! Rise now, and stand beside me."

Mayhew did so. The Spider clapped his hands, and his attendants returned.

"Take this man," he directed them, "and clothe him in black tights and a black jersey like unto mine, and a sword and pouch on an iron chain. And give him an apartment next to mine."

So Mayhew was led away, and duly bathed and clothed and fed. Then, in a small cave which he was informed was to be his, he lay down on luxurious rugs to sleep. But before he slept he resolved that he would use his new position to work the undoing of this monster who menaced the race which had befriended him.

HE WAS awakened by an attendant with a lighted torch. How long he had slept he had no means of knowing, for all hours of the day and night seem alike when one is living underground; but he felt thoroughly rested, and the attendant informed him that it was morning.

Breakfast was served him in his quarters.

Then the attendant brought him shears, a razor, hot water, soap and a polished steel mirror. Mayhew, fearful lest some one might recognize him without his bushy blond beard, merely trimmed it into some semblance of neatness and regularity.

Word was brought that the Spider wished to see him, and he was led into the presence of his excellency.

"Stand by my right hand," the creature snapped. Then, when Mayhew had taken the invited position, "Have you traveled much, Tolofo?"

Mayhew did some quick thinking, but could form no idea of what he might be letting himself in for. When in doubt, tell the truth. Mayhew did so.

"Excellency," said he, "I have sailed this sea, and have landed on many of its shores, including the continent which has no name. But never have I visited any part of Mu, other than the City of Gold."

"So you have visited the continent which has no name? Um! Some day I shall have you take me there, if you have the brain to learn worluk. Also there may be parts of the Golden City which you can penetrate for me. Let us begin at once. Bring me that globe, and place it at the foot of the throne."

Mayhew brought the crystal sphere, on its black pedestal. The Spider leaned forward, brushed one taloned hand across his parchment forehead, and then gazed intently into the limpid depths. A white-fanged smile broke across his thin, cruel lips.

"My, what a perfect specimen," he breathed. "Look, Tolofo, can you see what I see?"

Mayhew stared steadily into the crystal globe, then ran his fingers through his sandy hair.

"Excellency, I see nothing," he was forced to admit.

"Place the fingertips of your left hand upon my brow."

The young man did so. At once the clear glass clouded to a milky, pearly hue, which then began to whirl and churn like the lava of Pele. In the midst of this iridescent confusion there appeared a shapeless black blob.

"It looks like a spider," said Mayhew, feeling that some remark was expected.

The sinister monarch laughed.

"It is not, but it soon shall be," he cackled. Then clapping his hands, he commanded, "Bring the worluk powder."

Attendants came running in with a flat iron bowl, which they placed on the cavern floor before the throne. Then one of them plucked a torch from its niche in the wall and dipped the lighted end into the bowl. The contents began to smoke, a thick white cloud, which rose only to a height of ten or twelve feet, and then stopped abruptly, to rise no further.

THE SPIDER brushed Mayhew to one side. Then, gripping the arm of the throne with his left hand, he extended his right hand toward the pillar of smoke, and began to wave his fingers at it.

As if actually carved and shaped by the motions of that claw-like hand, the smoke bulged and solidified into a perfect sphere, which then gradually cleared until it became hazily translucent, resembling a huge ball of glass draped with a thin net of gray gauze.

The Spider scowled, and concentrated an intent stare upon this huge sphere, still weaving his fingers before him. Mayhew gasped, for a picture was taking shape within this immense gazing-crystal of smoke, a picture like the formless mass which he had just seen in the lesser crystal, when his fingertips had been pressed to the brow of the Spider.

The black blob formed, but now Mayhew could discern what it was. It was the back view of the naked torso and head of a man—a black man—seated on some steps in the courtyard of a Muian house. Every detail became as distinct as though the scene were actually located within the cavern throne room, separated from the watchers only by a thin and transparent drapery.

The Spider hissed a sharp command, "Bring me two of my most powerful assassins, armed with small clubs." Then to Mayhew, "I shall show you how we recruit our slaves."

Two burly yellow brutes came running, each holding in his right hand a leather covered metal billy.

"You see that Negro?" directed the Spider, pointing to the vision. "I want him, silently and unharmed."

The two thugs gave the customary Roman salute; then, to the intense surprise of the American, they dashed through the curtain of haze which separated the throne room from the garden scene. The Negro, as though startled by some slight sound, quickly turned his head, but down crashed two clubs on his upturned brow and he slumped insensible to the pavement of the courtyard.

Quickly and lithely the two yellow men dragged the black body through the curtain, to the foot of the throne, and again saluted their ruler. He waved his hand as though brushing away something; then ran his fingers tiredly across his eyes, and sank back upon his red marble throne. The ball of smoke and its vision faded and vanished. But the Negro still lay sprawled before them.

"That," announced the Spider wearily, "is worluk. But it is very exhausting." Then, to the two assassins, who were standing expectant, "Take him to the tunnel gangs."

Their faces fell. Probably they had been hoping to see this choice morsel fed to the eternal fires of Pele.

As the two yellow men picked up the still unconscious Negro, Mayhew got his first good view of the black man's face, and had difficulty in suppressing a gasp of recognition. For the Negro was Moorfi, faithful Moorfi, who had been his servant in the household of Julo.

"A favor, most gracious excellency," he said. "I am much impressed with the splendid physique of the slave. May I have him for my personal attendant?"

The Spider looked at Mayhew with a queer look.

"Did you not recognize the scene?"

"No."

"It was the courtyard of the house of Julo, whom you hate because he was the magistrate who sentenced you. Do you not fear a servant of Julo?"

That was so. In his guise as Tolofo, Mayhew was supposed to hate Julo, actually his friend and benefactor.

"This Negro may never have heard of me. I will sound him out!"

"Very well. But you take a dangerous chance. Be careful, for you are likely to prove of value to me."

So the Negro was carried away to Mayhew's quarters.

ATTENDANTS BROUGHT the Spider a large goblet, from which he drank.

"Have some?" he proffered. "It's sea water, my favorite liquor. Besides being very refreshing, my partaking of it symbolizes the union of Ocean and Pele, which I hope some day to accomplish."

Mayhew shook his head.

"I thank your excellency," he said, "but one who has sailed as much as I have grows to dislike salt water."

The Spider frowned at him. The frown became a diabolical leer. The taloned hands clutched the two arms of the throne. The yellow face became livid, then gray. The little squat, hunched-up frame shook and quivered, as with some intense emotion.

Mayhew stepped back aghast, and as he did so the Spider rose from his seat, and, with a gurgling gulp, flung himself at the retreating American.

But the move was feebly made. The monarch slumped to the

floor and rolled over onto his back, where he lay sprawled out, with his head painfully twisted and his eyes staring wide and sightlessly above him. His whole body flopped and twitched like a fish in the bottom of a boat. His thin lips, drawn back over sharp fangs, were flecked with pink foam, which pulsated and bubbled in unison with his groans.

The attendants fled shrieking.

Quick as a flash Mayhew sensed the trouble. One of his shipmates on the barque Alaska had been subject to just such seizures. It was epilepsy.

So, gingerly approaching the writhing creature, he turned it over onto its belly, whipped off his own jersey, folded it up, and placed it beneath the creature's face to ease the pounding of the crooked features against the hard stone floor of the cavern.

Then he held the body from rolling over in its convulsions, and waited. There was nothing else to do.

Gradually the paroxysms subsided, and the slaty cheeks resumed their normal yellow hue. The Spider coughed and spat, then nodded his head feebly and smiled a sickly smile.

"Your excellency is all right again," said Mayhew in an encouraging tone.

The Spider pushed himself into a sitting posture by means of his long arms and nodded his head.

"Support me," he said. "Kneel down behind me, and let me lean against you."

Mayhew did as directed. It required all his self-control to suppress a shudder of revulsion as that obscene body rested upon his breast.

For a few moments the Spider lay back and panted.

After a while Mayhew suggested, "I think your excellency is now well enough to stand up and return to the throne."

The vulture head turned on its short neck and regarded him over one shoulder with a wry smile.

"So you don't know?" said the Spider. "I thought that every

one knew. I shall never be well enough to stand. Pick me up and carry me to my throne."

So this world menace was a helpless cripple! A warped but mighty mind, in a warped and impotent body!

MAYHEW PICKED it up in his powerful arms and sprawled it back upon its skull-topped crimson throne.

The Spider regarded him with a look of almost kindness and gratitude.

"You alone, Tolofo," he said, "did not flee in terror from my seizure. I did well when I chose you to stand at my right hand."

"How often do you have these attacks?" asked Mayhew, with real concern in his voice.

"Sometimes two a day. Sometimes not once in many moons."

"May I make a suggestion?"

"Speak."

"Give up the sea water. I had a friend once who had the same trouble, and he found that too much salt always brought it on."

An expression of sadness passed across the frightful face of the Spider.

"I wonder if this symbolizes the failure of my great venture," he mused.

Then his mood changed, and he clapped his hands. Attendants came slinking back shamefacedly.

"I am tired," the monarch announced, "and I would have diversion. Bring me a maiden."

A few minutes later a yellow Oriental girl was led into the cavern. She was daintily and exquisitely formed. The tips of her firm young breasts were covered with tiny cones of burnished steel. From a belt of steel links there hung a loincloth of flaming scarlet. Steel bracelets encircled her perfect arms and legs. Her dark hair was done in a knot, and fastened with many skewers of steel. And she exhaled a perfume of water-heliotrope.

She walked into the room with an air of timidity, mingled with quiet dignity and pride, which clearly indicated that she knew that she had been chosen that day from among the slave girls to be the bride of the great king.

But it was a king whom she had never seen. As her eyes fell upon that squat creature, sprawled upon his blood-red throne, her face went stark with horror, her fingers curled and tensed and were brought up before her mouth, and then she slumped pitifully to the floor, where she lay sobbing.

"So you don't like me, eh?" snarled the Spider, his lip curling. "You're afraid of me, eh? I'm repulsive to you, am I? Well, I'll *make* you like me. Stand up!"

But she only groaned and sobbed the harder.

Two attendants pulled her to her feet, but she hung limp between them.

"Look at me!"

But she hung her head and averted her gaze.

One of the two attendants slapped her smartly across the face. Mayhew tensed. This was going too far.

CHAPTER XII

THE SPIDER STRIKES

THE SPIDER TURNED his vulture face slowly around toward the young man. An inscrutable smile played across his features.

"Curb your natural chivalry for a moment," he said, "and you will see that I mean the maiden no harm." Then to the attendants, "Slap her again!"

One of them did so. The beautiful yellow girl opened her eyes and stared at the mad monarch for an instant. With a quick gesture he extended his right hand toward her, its fingers rigid, and waved it with a slight quiver. Instantly her body stiffened and her stare became fixed and vacant. The two attendants let go of her, and she stood alone.

"Come, my dear," cooed the Spider, in as seductive a voice as he was capable of.

Like a sleepwalker she advanced to the throne. She crawled into the lap of the repulsive creature seated there. She laid her cheek against his with a contented little sigh, and began running her slim fingers caressingly over his face and head and arms.

"I would be alone," he said simply, and Adams Mayhew and the other attendants left the room.

At his quarters, Mayhew found the huge Negro sitting up and staring stupidly around. Not a sign of recognition did Moorfi give him.

Mayhew closed the door and said in a low voice, "Quiet, now, and show no surprise. I am Adams Mayhew."

The Negro arose incredulously.

Finally he smiled and said, "For the love of the good Ra, I believe you're right. But what are you doing here?"

"Spying on the Spider. He thinks that I am Tolofo, a fugitive from Julo's justice. Have you ever heard of Tolofo?"

"Can't say that I ever have."

"Well, stick to that story. Are Julo and Marta well?"

"Perfectly."

"And Eleria?"

The Negro grinned.

"Nicely too. But she won't have anything to do with Porto. Still thinks you and he are the same fellow."

"So Porto is safe? Did he tell what happened at Tirio's castle?"

"Only to Julo. 'Fraid any one else would think he was crazy with all this talk of spider-men appearing and disappearing and all that. And as for your disappearing, that story certainly wouldn't be believed, for every one knows that you and Porto are the same fellow. And now you're somebody else, again. Can't you be yourself for a little while?"

"I'm afraid I'm doomed to spend the rest of my life in one impersonation after another," Mayhew wryly replied.

"Well, doesn't it beat all! It reminds me of a story of two sea-captains—"

But Mayhew cut off the narrative with, "And what has become of that rat-faced centurion?"

"Oh, Tirio's back running around the city again. He and Porto called off the blood feud, on account of having fought the spider-men together. But how did you get here?"

"The same way you did."

"And how is that? I was unconscious when it happened."

"It's a long story. Keep your eyes open, and you may learn how. You are to be my servant while we're here."

"While we're here?" quoted Moorfi with a grimace. "No one ever gets out of the clutches of the Spider."

"I mean to," said Mayhew grimly. Then, "Does Eleria see much of Tirio?"

"No, she doesn't speak to him either. But sooner or later she'll make up with either him or Porto, and then the blood feud will be on again. They're both in love with her."

Mayhew groaned.

"Just think!" he exclaimed. "Here am I, and Eleria is a hundred miles away with those two men."

"You wouldn't want her to be here, would you?"

And Adams Mayhew, remembering what he had just seen in the throne room of the Spider, answered an emphatic, "No!"

Then he cautioned Moorfi always to address him as "Tolofo." A slight slip of the tongue by the faithful black, and he and his master might both go to feed the eternal fires of Pele.

EVIDENTLY THE little yellow girl kept the Spider amused for the rest of that day, for he did not again send for Adams Mayhew.

But the following day, and for many days thereafter, the supposed Tolofo was in attendance on his sovereign a large part of the time. And always he sought to ingratiate himself, and to learn as much as he could of the methods and plans of the sinister Spider.

Daily he practiced worluk, until whenever he pressed his finger tips on the brow of his patron, he was able to see in the crystal globe whatever the Spider envisioned there. Sometimes he would even almost succeed in forming visions of his own, but they never were quite distinct, nor could he ever completely shape the gray smoke from the iron bowl.

The Spider also offered to teach him how to tame the yellow girls of the harem, and how to bend their wills to his pleasure, but this Mayhew refused to try. And, although the Spider obscenely twitted him for his chivalry, the old creature did not press the point. But Mayhew did see many beautiful maidens come before the Spider and recoil from their fate in stark horror, only to be reduced to doll-like automatons by a few waves of his taloned hand.

By means of the mind and memory of the Spider, projected into the crystal gazing-globe, Adams Mayhew paid optical visits to many parts of the empire of Mu. And often when the ball of transparent smoke was formed, he witnessed assassinations and kidnapings.

But he learned that this powerful alchemist whom he served was limited and hampered in many ways. The Spider could see in the crystal sphere, and contact by means of the ball of smoke, only such places as he had formerly visited in the flesh. And not even all of those, but only such as had particularly impressed themselves upon him when he had visited them. Also, although he could project his minions through the curtain of worluk smoke into actual presence in the scenes which he was envisioning, yet he could not pass through the smoke-screen himself.

And his infirmity kept him pretty well tied down to the throne room cavern and his adjoining quarters. It was almost pathetic how he longed to travel, to visit parts of the world which he had never seen, and in particular to visit other parts of the continent of Mu. This longing would have been actually pathetic, had it been due to a desire to mingle with his fellow men. But it was actuated by a fiendish wish to extend his occult power by adding to the spots which he could summon to sight in the visions of his crystal globe, and into which he could launch his assassins through the medium of the magic smoke.

Moorfi was occasionally present, in attendance on his master, at some of these séances, but Mayhew kept him away as much as possible, lest he make some break which would reveal to the Spider Mayhew's true identity. The reason which Mayhew gave to the Spider, however, was that Moorfi might see an attack on some former friend of his, and attempt to interfere. This explanation not only served to excuse Moorfi's absence, but also still further established Mayhew's devotion to the cause. And this was to come in very handy at a later date.

ONE DAY, after the American had become proficient in reading the Spider's crystal-visions, by the mental rapport induced by the pressure of finger tips of the one on the brow of the other, the mad monarch summoned him to attend one of his daily séances.

"Ah, Tolofo," remarked the Spider, "touch my forehead quickly, if you would see a most beautiful girl. Of course, I know that you are cold to the charms of the little darlings of my own yellow race. But here is a white beauty, who will quicken even your sluggish pulse."

Mayhew shrugged his shoulders and placed the tips of the fingers of his left hand upon the brow of his patron. The crystal-clear globe clouded with a pearly haze, which straightway began to swirl twist before his eyes, soon becoming a kaleidoscopic vortex of peacock hues.

Then gradually the vision cleared and took form. It was a street scene in the Golden City.

And in the midst of the street stood the beautiful Eleria!

Adams Mayhew gasped, and his fingers trembled on the brow of the Spider. The latter leered up at him, and said, "I thought that that would interest even you. Shall I send for her through the ball of smoke, to be a plaything for you here in these dismal caves?"

What could Mayhew reply? He could not disclaim his interest, which had been all too evident. He certainly did not wish to subject Eleria to captivity here; but, on the other hand, neither did he wish to leave her in the Golden City within reach of his two rivals.

As his mind struggled to frame an appropriate answer to the offer of the Spider, the latter suddenly pushed Mayhew away, and shouted, "Quick! Bring worluk. He comes! The man whom I have been seeking these many moons."

The vision swirled and vanished. Gone was Eleria. But also, with this swift shift of the mad monarch's mood, was gone the necessity of replying to his question.

Slaves came running with the iron bowl of powder, which they promptly ignited. The smoke billowed upward, and took shape at the wave of a clawlike hand. The same street scene appeared in the midst of the smoke, with Eleria still standing there.

But there was one addition. Down the street toward her was swaggering the rat-faced Tirio, in his blue bordered centurion's tunic. Eleria was smiling, and seemed glad to see the newcomer, who saluted and stopped to chat with her.

Mayhew set his jaw and clenched his fists, and the Spider, glancing up at him for an instant, grinned approval.

But then the centurion began to move away.

The Spider clapped his hands in command, and shrieked, "Where are those assassins? Why aren't they here? My man escapes me!"

Attendants scattered to seek out the cause of the delay, but no assassins appeared.

"Quick, Tolofo, you!" shrieked the Spider. "Into the smoke and seize him for me!"

And such was the hypnotic power of that command that Mayhew leaped forward without thought or hesitation; and, passing through the curtain of smoke, he grappled with his old enemy.

THE CAVERN throne room vanished, and Mayhew was back in the Golden City. And, as on the day of his first arrival there, he was engaged in a hand-to-hand combat with Tirio, the centurion.

Although his onslaught had taken his enemy completely by surprise, yet the latter fought with the ferocity of a cornered rat. In a few minutes Mayhew was down on his back, with Tirio sitting astride him, the hands of each locked on the arms of the other.

"What's the matter with you?" Tirio panted. "Who are you, with your bushy yellow beard, and that strange black costume? I've seen your face before, hut your beard hides most of it. You look like Porto, but he was clean-shaven yesterday. If you are Porto, desist; for the blood feud is off."

For reply, Mayhew gave a heave, and the struggle resumed. Tirio reached for his sword. But a warning shout, "Beware, Tolofo!" came from the air above. Mayhew had a momentary vision of a yellow man in a red tunic stooping down and snatching the blade from Tirio's hand.

Tirio blanched.

"So you are Tolofo," he gasped, "turned spider-man, and come back for revenge. I swear that it wasn't I who framed that case against you. Help! Police!"

Mayhew thought of the Biblical proverb, "The wicked flee when no man pursueth," and smiled grimly. So it was Tirio who had been responsible for the undeserved exile of the dead overseer. One more debt which the rat-faced one must be made to pay! But how could this ever be accomplished?

Quite a crowd had gathered by now. Eleria was no longer in evidence. In a moment the police would be here, in response to Tirio's frantic calls for help.

Then the supposed Tolofo would have to go back to jail; and if he should declare himself to be Adams Mayhew, this disclosure would in no way diminish the hatred of the centurion, who would take great pains that word of the prisoner's true identity should not get out. Mayhew was in a fix. The only solution seemed to be to kill his opponent before help came, for with the death of Tirio would die all suspicion that Mayhew was the escaped convict, Tolofo. So, with grim desperation, he clutched now for Tirio's throat.

And then he felt a strange inexplicable pull on him, as from a gigantic magnet. As he wrestled with his opponent, each turn and twist and roll seemed to carry the two of them further up the street toward the spot from which the American had first launched his attack. The crowd receded as they rolled.

He heard gruff shouts, "Make way!"

The crowd parted. And then Tirio got his hands on Mayhew's

throat. Mayhew's wind was completely cut off. He gasped and strained for breath. A red haze spread over his vision. No longer did he feel the magnetic pull.

Then the hands of his opponent were torn from his throat, and his opponent's body was dragged off of him. With great painful sobs the air came back into his tortured lungs. His vision cleared. Yet still the red color of surrounding objects persisted.

For he was lying on the floor of the throne room cavern of the Spider. His enemy, held in the clutches of two burly yellow brutes, was staring with wide-mouthed horror at the scene.

"Take him away!" waved the Spider. Then to Mayhew, "You did a good job, Tolofo; but if I hadn't sent one of my men to seize Tirio's sword, you would have been done for."

"I thank your excellency for saving my life," breathed Mayhew, getting to his feet and gently feeling of his neck where his opponent's hands had been. "What do you plan to do with the victim? Feed him to the eternal flames of Pele?"

Mayhew grinned as he said this. Not because of any personal joy at thus getting rid of his enemy and rival, for he would take no pleasure in the cold blooded slaughter of even such a one as Tirio; but rather because there suddenly flashed through his mind a realization of irony of playing off against each other these two enemies of the government, so each would destroy the other.

But the Spider's reply suddenly shocked him out of his complacency.

It was, "Certainly not! Haven't I told you that I have been trying for many moons to get him here, so that I can propose an alliance to him?"

Instead of having helped the government of Mu, Mayhew had assisted in what might prove to be its undoing! The only crumb of comfort to this situation was that he had at least separated Tirio and Eleria.

"Well," announced the Spider, "let's do some more fishing."

And he stared again into the crystal globe.

AT THAT instant one of the attendants announced a man, seeking audience; and the Spider commanded that the man be brought in. The newcomer was small and yellow, but well muscled. He carried a spear.

After the customary Roman salute he looked askance at Mayhew and said, "I'd rather not have him present. What I have to say is for the ears of your excellency alone."

"You will speak in the presence of any one I choose to have present," snapped the Spider. "Proceed."

Still looking at Mayhew furtively out of the corner of his eye, the man said, "But, your excellency, what I have to say is that this fellow beside you is *not* Tolofo, but an impostor!"

All this while, Mayhew had been racking his brains to identify the man, whose face seemed strangely familiar.

Meanwhile the Spider was snarling his reply, "That is a rash charge, Koko; and, if you cannot substantiate it, it will mean for you the fate to which you have pushed so many others." Then, turning to Mayhew, "What say you, Tolofo?"

The Spider's remarks had finally given the American his clue. This man was the one who had quarreled with Tolofo over his kindness to Adams Mayhew.

Mayhew shrugged his shoulders as he replied, "It is what I might expect from Koko, your excellency. He and I never got along together during all the time that we were spearmen at the eternal fires of Pele. I have heard rumors that he jealously resented my promotion to foremanship, and again when you honored me by elevating me to this post by your side."

"Koko," snapped the Spider. "Where did you get this insane idea?"

"In a message from one of Tolofo's own squad at the excavations, your excellency. The message stated that Tolofo is dead, and that this person at your side is none other than the slave, Adamo Mayho."

"What say you, Tolofo?"

Again Mayhew shrugged his shoulders, as he replied, "I tried to be fair and merciful to my men, your excellency. Several of them, misinterpreting my kindness, approached me to let them go over the hill. Naturally I refused. This yarn is probably revenge for that refusal. Also possibly an attempt to implicate me, before I report them."

"You should have reported the episode at once when it happened, Tolofo," snapped the Spider.

"Your excellency, the episode occurred the night before I was summoned here. I overlooked it in the excitement of moving."

"Very well. Your explanations are satisfactory. As for this lying troublemaker of a Koko, take him away and lock him up—until we hear from the slave who started the accusation. He, the slave, is to be sent for at once."

The informer wilted and was dragged away. And an ominous gloom settled over Adams Mayhew.

But the Spider did not notice this change in the mien of his favorite, for he at once turned his interrupted attention back to the gazing-sphere.

"Your fingers!" he commanded.

And Adams Mayhew once more established rapport with the mind of his patron. Once more the limpid depths curdled, then swirled, then cleared, this time disclosing the courtyard of the house of Julo. As they gazed beautiful Eleria entered the scene. Her cameo face was, distrait, her dainty hands clasped upon her breast, and she was panting.

JULO—SUAVE, MAJESTIC and kindly—entered the courtyard. Excitedly the girl rushed over to him, placed both her hands upon his shoulders and looked up appealingly into his face. Of course, the two watchers could not hear what she was saying, but it was evident that she was recounting the abduction of Tirio which she had recently witnessed.

"Once more this pearl of a white girl plays into our hands," announced the Spider gleefully. "Once more she lures a victim into my web. Quick, the worluk, and four assassins!"

"But, your excellency," objected Mayhew, horrified, "surely you do not plan to kill that girl! What has she ever done to you?"

The Spider grinned as he replied, "No, no. Merely Julo. He is an enemy who has long escaped me."

Mayhew groaned inwardly. Here was his best friend about to be slaughtered, and he was powerless to prevent it.

The assassins arrived. The bowl of powder was brought and lighted. The globe of transparent smoke was formed by a few waves of the alchemist's hands. Julo's back was turned.

"Go get him!" hissed the Spider, and the four thugs, with daggers up-raised, leapt from the red-lit cavern into the court-yard of Julo.

But after them leapt Adams Mayhew.

"Kataka, Julo!" he shouted, shoving the nearest assassin aside.

Julo turned, just in time to seize the wrist of one descending dagger hand. Then he and Mayhew and the four spider-men went down together in a heap.

"Help!" shouted Julo, and black servants came running.

One of them seized Mayhew and dragged him off the heap.

"Don't you know me?" gasped the American. "I'm Adams Mayhew. Let me alone, and help Julo."

"You're one of these vanishing spider-men, that what you are," retorted the Negro, "and I'm helping my master right how by keeping you off of him." He lunged at Mayhew. In self-defense, the latter was forced to grapple with him. But the American was no match for the black, who quickly got the upper hand.

Then once, again Mayhew felt the magnetic drawing force of the will of the Spider, slowly causing him to ooze out from beneath the body of the Negro, and to rematerialize in the red-lit throne room of the volcanic caverns.

He had saved Julo—that is, he hoped he had—and now he was being pulled back to the lair of the Spider, there to pay the penalty for thwarting the plans of the monster. Doubtless he would speedily be thrown to Pele, and this time there would be no escape.

CHAPTER XIII

MU STRIKES BACK

STRANGE TO RELATE, more than he feared for his own fate, Mayhew regretted that all the spying which he had done on the plans of the Spider would now go to waste. And also that he would never see Eleria again.

So with all his might he clung to the body of the Negro, and opposed his own will-power to that of the Spider, striving desperately not to be sucked back through the ball of smoke into the cavern, where sat the monster on his skull-topped, blood-red throne.

But, despite his efforts both physical and mental, the sunlight gradually became a reddish glare, the weight of the black body upon him gradually became more tenuous and unreal. He could even dimly see the squat figure of the Spider, Seated on his crimson marble throne, his arms stretched out, pulling Adams Mayhew back into his clutches.

Then something snapped. The figure on the throne pitched forward toward him, a fishy, vacant look upon its face. The cavern faded. The sunlight reappeared. Adams Mayhew was lying on the flagging of the courtyard of Julo's home, beneath a burly Negro who was trying to throttle him.

"Get up!" snapped an authoritative voice. "Get up, Tombi. What have you there?"

At the same instant Mayhew felt a tug at his waist.

"Watch out, sir," the Negro replied. "This is a spider-man, and he's armed."

The priests hurled him
onto the sacrificial stone

"I'm watching out," said the voice, "and I've taken his sword. Get up."

The Negro cautiously let go of Mayhew and got to his feet. Mayhew also rose, and faced the frowning Julo.

"Well," said the latter, smiling grimly, "at last we have secured a specimen. That is, unless suddenly you vanish like the rest."

"Get me out of here, and into some bedroom," Mayhew urged, "and then I'll not vanish. The Spider has no power in places where he has never been."

And he made a dash for one of the surrounding doorways.

A Negro stepped to intercept him, but Julo commanded, "Let him go, and follow."

Safely within the room Mayhew halted, and panted, "He can send his assassins in here from the courtyard, but he cannot drag me back, and they can expect no aid from him while out of his sight."

"But who are you?" asked Julo, with a puzzled frown.

"I'm Adams Mayhew."

Julo walked over and inspected him carefully. Then burst into a laugh, a rather sheepish one.

"I believe you are, at that," said he. "Well, of all the amazing turns of fate! Eleria, come and see who's here. It's an old friend of yours."

But there was no reply.

"Where is Eleria?" Julo demanded of the servants, but she was nowhere to be found.

Suddenly a realization dawned on Adams Mayhew. The assassins of the Spider had taken her back with them. He sank to a bench and held his face in his hands. For he was thinking of the fate, which he had witnessed, of the little, yellow girls in the harem of the Spider, and he was picturing the same fate meted out to Eleria!

AT LENGTH he roused himself and turned a haggard face to Julo, who stood looking down at him with deep and kindly concern.

"I know," said the magistrate. "You don't need to tell me. Our little friend has vanished with the spider-men. Perhaps she has gone to the fate from which you have just saved me."

"Worse than that, sir," replied Mayhew soberly. Then briefly he sketched the hypnotic love-powers of the Spider.

"Well, you have seen the creature face to face, and have survived," said Julo. "Others can do the same."

"But that doesn't save Eleria," gloomily replied the American.

"Maybe it does. Tell me all you know, and then we can make our plans."

So Mayhew rapidly sketched what he knew of the personality, powers, forces and ambitions of the Spider, together with his own history since his disappearance from the castle of Tirio. Julo had already learned from Moorfi of the original kidnaping, and from Porto of the fighting at the castle.

When Mayhew concluded, Julo clapped him on the shoulder, and said, "Well, at last we know who, what and where the Spider is. You have brought us more information as the result of a few months' work on your part, than the entire secret service of the

Empire of Mu has been able to glean in as many years. Let me congratulate you."

"You say you know who the Spider is. Who is he?"

"Many years ago, shortly before we began to hear rumors of the menace of the Spider, a paralyzed hunchback, a great scientist, of the yellow race, visited this city, to demand from the government a high official position, in recognition of his scientific attainments. I remember his calling at my house, and being carried into the courtyard. His request was refused and, threatening reprisals, he went back to his own city. Soon thereafter his death was reported, and the government breathed more easily, for he was a brilliant man with considerable of a personal following. But it now appears that he did not die."

"But what about Eleria?"

"Fortunately Mu and Eleria can be served by the same move. I shall organize a secret force and attack his stronghold. You can act as our guide. We shall move first to the fjord where you labored as a slave. There we shall put a stop to his excavations. I can't imagine what they are for, but undoubtedly their purpose is sinister. Then you can lead us to the shaft which gives entrance to his underground domains. Through that shaft we shall enter, put an end to the Spider, and rescue Eleria. Now that we know the source and nature of his powers, they need no longer terrify us."

"He may possess other powers."

"You saw no indications of any in all the months that you were with him?"

"No."

"And his forces appear to be small?"

"Yes. Very small."

"Then on with the attack!"

Mayhew next gave his host a list of all the places in the city which he remembered having seen through the crystal globe of the Spider.

For fear that information of Mayhew's return might eventually find its way to the ears of the enemy, he was taken to the jail and locked up there under the name of Tolofo. But many were the conferences held in his cell.

Thither, among others, came Porto. At first he and Mayhew were rather cool to each other, but one day Julo got the two of them together, and spoke to them in a fatherly way.

He said, "You are both in love with Eleria." They glared at each other. "And so is Tirio." They glared at Julo. "And so most likely is the Spider. In fact, it is hard to conceive of any one not succumbing to the charms of so exquisite a creature as she is." A look of horror spread over both of their faces. "I fancy that either of you would rather the other should get her, than to have her fall prey to the Spider, or to his ally Tirio." They nodded. "Then, by the name of Ra, shake hands, and promise each other to stand by the winner against all the world. And may the best man win."

They did so. Porto the Muian and Adams Mayhew the American then became fast friends, although avowed rivals for the hand of Eleria.

Mayhew continued to wear his beard, lest the Spider catch sight of him shaven in the crystal globe, and thus might learn that Adamo Mayho was not dead.

AT LAST the night arrived for the departure of the expedition. Under cover of darkness, Mayhew was smuggled out of the jail and aboard ship. The jail-keeper was instructed to give out word that Tolofo had escaped, for it might later be necessary for Mayhew again to impersonate the dead overseer. He was seen only by the men who shared the same boat with him, and to them he was introduced by his right name, or rather by its Muian variant, "Adamo Mayho."

Two nights later they reached the naval rendezvous off the coast just north of the volcano. There were several hundred boats of the prevailing Muian type, long and low, with triangular, awning-striped sails. These boats, in all, held many picked men.

Although there were many deep fjords along this volcanic northern coast, Mayhew's detailed description of the place where he had worked had led his friends to believe that they

"Oh, Ra," sang the priest, "shine thy approval on this offering which we bring to thee!"

Mayhew watched the knife, knowing that when the ray reached the position above his heart, his chest would be opened with one swift stroke

could identify the particular chasm. So they drew in close to shore near where they supposed the camp to be, and sent Mayhew with a small party to reconnoiter. It proved to be the correct place, so the party returned to the beach to report, and Mayhew by prearrangement went on alone.

Skirting the headquarters, which was wrapped in slumber, he proceeded until he came to the cave which he had formerly occupied as overseer. It was rather isolated from the rest of the camp, so, without fear of arousing any one but its inmate, he knocked loudly on its door.

After repeated rappings, a sleepy voice inquired, "Who comes?"

"A messenger from headquarters."

"In the name of Pele, what do you want at this late hour of night?"

"I am sent by his excellency to take over your job, and am instructed to stay with you until the transfer has been arranged."

"Have you brought written authority with you?"

"I have."

"Then slip it under the door."

In preparation for just such a request, Mayhew's friends in the Golden City had prepared an appropriate order on parchment, copying the spider-crest and the style of printing from one of the notices which the Spider himself had caused to be posted in the city. The language of the order was largely based upon Mayhew's recollection of the language of similar orders during his term of service with the Spider. Also Mayhew was clad in a careful copy, made from memory, of the spider-crested red tunic, worn by members of the enemy order. But in a bundle he carried a tunic of plain design, for use later in the night.

There were sounds of striking a light within the cave. Then illumination glowed around the edges of the door. Mayhew pushed the parchment underneath and a few moments later heard the sliding of bolts. The door opened and a man peered out.

"Well, well," he boomed. "My old friend, Tolofo! So you have come back to take over the job from which I ousted you. Well, turn about is fair play. Come on in. I hope that I do as well by myself, when I return to his excellency, as you did; but probably it will be just my luck to go back to guarding the fires of Pele. Come in, and make yourself at home."

MAYHEW HAD never seen the man who superseded him. But it was evident that this jovial yellow person had been a friend of Tolofo's and a spearman of Pele. With that to start on, and by being rather guarded in his conversation, he could doubtless escape detection until an opportunity presented itself to slip a knife between this fellow's ribs.

Ugh! He shuddered at the thought of killing in cold blood, and especially such a friendly soul as this! The man appeared to have been a close intimate of Tolofo, and hence probably a decent sort. And now Mayhew must strike down, unarmed and unwarned, the friend of his friend. Every atom of his nature recoiled from the task, yet it was necessary for the cause—and for Eleria.

At the thought of her he shuddered again.

The overseer, noticing this, said, "You are cold, good Tolofo, let me pour you some wine and throw a sleeping mat over your shoulders. The night is damp, and you have come a long way. Have you eaten?"

This was too much! He was to eat and drink at his victim's table, and be tenderly cared for by him. But he must—for Eleria. Chivalry to an enemy has no place when a woman's honor is at stake. Mayhew sat down heavily on a stool by the table.

The yellow man closed and barred the door.

"You seem tired as well as cold," he said in a friendly voice, "but soon I'll have you fixed all right."

He waddled over to a closet, from which he produced a jug and two goblets. These he placed on the table.

"Help yourself," he jovially invited, "while I get you that mat I promised you."

Mayhew poured a glass of wine and raised it to his lips; then hesitated. This was too much! The fellow was being too kind! Mayhew could not drink his wine and then cut him down in cold blood. There must be some other alternative.

With these thoughts he swung suddenly around to face his host. And it was well that he did so, for there stood the man, with dagger upraised, behind Mayhew's stool.

Just in time the American threw himself sidewise to the floor, and down came the dagger, driven deep into the table. The wine jug overturned and gurgled its contents out onto the table top, thence in a narrow stream to the edge and off onto the floor. The stool rolled into a corner.

Catlike, Mayhew sprang to his feet—he had learned that from being knocked into the scuppers aboard the barque Alaska. Drawing his broad-sword he rushed the spider-man. A fierce exultation thrilled him; no longer was it necessary for him to kill in cold blood!

But the other man stepped nimbly back to the wall, snatched his own sword from where its belt and scabbard hung from a peg, and leaped forward again to meet the onslaught of the American.

His agility belied his huge bulk. Parrying Mayhew's first stroke, he swept a return blow; and, as Mayhew stepped back to avoid it, the yellow man with a sudden turn of the wrist caught Mayhew's blade with his, wrenched it from his momentarily slackened grasp, and sent it hurtling into a corner. Then he charged again.

THERE WAS but one thing for the American to do. Instead of fleeing, he stepped in under the blow, planted his right fist in the fat belly of the overseer and seized the sword wrist with his own left hand.

The fat paunch, however, had plenty of muscle behind its rolls of flesh; so the blow only slightly winded the man. But, combined with a sudden wrench on his wrist, it was sufficient to cause him to drop his sword. Then the two men grappled.

The chunky yellow man not only outweighed the American, he also had more strength and more wrestling skill. And so it was not long before Adams Mayhew's right arm was "in chancery," pulled up behind his back with the hand opposite his shoulder blades. His opponent had him at his mercy, and could easily dislocate his shoulder at will.

Desperate, Mayhew lunged behind him with his left fist, but his opponent deftly caught it, and now had both of Mayhew's arms in chancery. Then the man began pushing him toward the table, where the dagger still stuck, imbedded in the wood. The purpose was evident. Mayhew braced his feet against the floor and strained backward, but the yellow man bunted him with his knee, forcing him forward.

The time for fighting was over; the time for temporizing and persuasion had arrived.

"What have you got against me?" asked Mayhew. "We used to be good friends."

"I've nothing at all against you," the other replied. "But I don't want you to get my job. My return to the court of his excellency might not result in promotion like yours did. And I've no intention of becoming a mere spearman again, if I can help it."

"But what excuse can you give for my death?"

"None; and I shan't have to. I'll heave your body into the fjord and say that you never arrived."

"It will go hard with you, if you are even suspected of my death, for I am a favorite of his excellency."

"It looks like it," sneered the other, "deprived of your soft job, and sent back here to be a foreman."

By this time they had arrived at the table. Mayhew was pushed against the edge, and then the upper part of his body was forced forward, until his chin touched the board. His captor then grasped both of his wrists with one fat hand and the other reached for the dagger.

It was Mayhew's last chance for life. Desperately he leaned his entire weight on the table and kicked backward with both feet.

The yellow man was not taken by surprise, however, and braced his own feet to withstand the shove. But he had forgotten the dripping wine. He was standing in a puddle of the slippery liquid, and his feet gave way and slid.

He grabbed the edge of the table to steady himself, and the combined pressure of himself and Mayhew pushed the table out from under, and the two of them crashed to the floor together.

Mayhew twisted around as he fell, thus landing on his back with his hands free; and, as the overseer came down on top of him, he drove his right fist squarely to the other's jaw. Then he scrambled to his feet and grabbed the knife.

The overseer slowly and groggily arose, blinked, shook his head, and then lunged forward with a bellow of rage. Mayhew met him with the point of the dagger to his left breast, and the fight was over.

The American drew a couple of deep breaths. But there was no time to lose, as some one might arrive at any moment. So he speedily set about putting the room in order.

FIRST HE dragged the body over to the pile of sleeping mats, placed it in a natural position with its back to the door, and covered all but its head with one of the mats. Then he rearranged the upset furniture and mopped up the blood and wine. He was just finishing when there came a peremptory rap on the door.

Stepping over to it, he softly asked, "Who comes?"

"It's the guard from headquarters, on a round of inspection," shouted the voice outside. "Why are your lights lit at this late hour of the night?"

Sliding back the bolts and opening the door a crack, Mayhew replied, "Sh! The overseer is asleep."

The guard entered, glanced at the recumbent figure on the sleeping mats, then stared at Mayhew.

"Then who are you?" he demanded.

"Sh!" the American again replied. "I am the new overseer. Here are my orders assigning me to the command of the third squad. They direct me to spend the night with the overseer of that squad."

The guard glanced at the paper, which it was evident he could not read, and then started to stuff it into his pouch; but Mayhew snatched it away, saying, "No, no! I need those to prove my identity."

"But why didn't you report at headquarters?" grumbled the guard.

"There were no lights there, so I thought I would wait until morning."

The guard departed, still grumbling. As soon as time enough had elapsed for him to complete his rounds, Mayhew took the keys of the dead overseer and set out for the cave which housed his former squad. At the grating he called softly the names of several of them, until at last a light was lit inside and one of the slaves came to the opening.

"By the holy name of Ra, see who's here!" the slave exclaimed. "It's our old pal, Adamo Mayho, come back to us!"

The others, thus aroused, crowded to the entrance. Mayhew checked them over. All his old squad was there, with the exception of one named Meeno; and there was one new face.

He was just about to ask, "What has become of Meeno?" when one of the slaves asked that same question of him.

Mayhew instantly grasped the situation, and replied in an offhand tone, "Oh, he is to be fed to Pele, for presuming to tell the Spider that I am not Tolofo." He paused to let this sink in; then, "But, as for the rest of you, I have returned to keep my promise to set you free."

"Three cheers—" began one of them.

But another clapped a hand over his mouth with a "Be still, you fool!"

Mayhew unlocked the grating and led them to his own cave, where he distributed swords and knives from his own clothes bundle and from the stock of the dead overseer. Mayhew donned a plain tunic.

He explained to them the plan of campaign, and they extinguished the lights and waited.

THEY HAD not long to wait, for soon they heard the sound of fighting farther down the ravine, as Julo's army fell upon the sleeping guardhouse and headquarters of the spider-men. Then Mayhew and his little group sallied forth. As each foreman, roused by the confusion, opened the door of his cave to investigate, he was cut down. Then his keys were obtained, and his squad was released to augment Mayhew's forces. Soon all the prisoners were free, and most of them were armed. They then took up a position, blocking the road which led to the volcano, and thus preventing the escape of any spider-men to warn the Spider.

In a few moments it was over; the enemy were wiped out to a man. Then began the silent and cautious advance up the trail, with Mayhew in the lead, showing the way. At this rate, they would reach the shaft, as planned, before daylight. They were jubilant.

But their jubilation was short-lived. As they were passing through a certain small crater-like pocket in the mountains, they began to smell sulphur. They gasped and sneezed. And then, from a thousand jets in the walls of rock, there burst upon them a perfect deluge of noxious gasses.

Mayhew was the first to sense the situation.

"Up! Up!" he urged. "Up the sides, every man of you!"

The orderly advance became a scrambled rout as the men fought their way up the rocky walls. The word "fought" is literally correct, for the men clawed and shoved at each other, forgetting friend and ally in their mad struggle for self-preservation.

Some of the jets of gas became ignited from the torches carried by the expedition. Several explosions were heard. Rocks began to roll down the precipitous cliffs. And molten fire began to pour from many jet-holes.

Adams Mayhew, panting and pain-racked, coughing and straining for breath, reached the top of one of the cliffs. He

glanced back down into the inclosure. The entire bowl was lit by
the red glare of the streams of lava, and the burning jets of gas,
so that he could see clearly the devastation below.

Hundreds of black forms lay huddled at the bottom of the
ravine, some crushed by rocks, some singed by fire, some twisted
into grotesque shapes by asphyxiation, and some still twitching
slightly with expiring life. But not a man was struggling upward.

Around the rim stood many spider-men, silhouettes of red
against the velvet sky, still rolling rocks down on those below.
Then a gust of poison fumes wafted up from the valley of death,
blinding and choking Mayhew, and he fled across the volcanic
rocks, away from that awful charnel-house.

CHAPTER XIV

ESCAPE?

HOW LONG OR where he ran, after the sudden destruction of the army of his friends, Mayhew never knew, for the last thing he remembered was turning blindly away from that awful holocaust. There followed a vague treadmill nightmare of stumbling interminably over volcanic rocks in the jet darkness of the night.

Then he awoke to find himself lying on the hard stone floor of a red-lit cavern. He stirred and groaned.

A voice above him hissed, "So, Tolofo, you have come back to me, eh?"

Blinking and rubbing his eyes, Mayhew looked up, to see the Spider leering down at him from his throne.

"Get up!" commanded the Spider.

Mayhew struggled to his feet and feebly gave the Roman salute. The Spider grinned.

"Still game," said he appreciatively; then, "Your friends in the Golden City didn't treat you very well, did they? I did my best to save you, but unfortunately I had one of my seizures just as I was dragging you back to safety through the ball of worluk smoke. Pretty forgiving of me, too, I call it."

"Wh-what was?" stuttered Mayhew, sparring for time.

"My trying to rescue you after you had impulsively spoiled my attack on our enemy Julo. But, of course, I can understand your eagerness to do the killing yourself."

Mayhew's head was beginning to clear, and gradually the astounding realization was being forced upon him that the

Spider had misinterpreted his rush through the ball of smoke as an attempt on his part to kill, rather than to rescue, his supposed enemy, Julo. Perhaps, then, the Spider did not suspect him of complicity in last night's happenings; or, more likely, the Spider was merely playing with him, as a cat with a mouse. Even so, the cat's play would mean a few more minutes of life.

The next question of the Spider went far toward solving Mayhew's problem.

"How did the Muians learn the location of my mountain stronghold? Did they extort this information out of you by torture?"

Mayhew drew himself up proudly, and said, with double entendre, "No one can get from me information which I do not choose to give."

"Good!" exclaimed the Spider. "I respect your loyalty. But how, then, did they find out?"

"I have an idea," Mayhew judiciously replied, "for there was a rumor around the prison that some fishermen had seen signs of suspicious activity along the north coast. Spies were sent from the secret service of Julo, to reconnoiter. These confirmed the suspicions, and so the expedition was dispatched."

The Spider thoughtfully nodded his vulture head.

"Yes," he said, "it sounds likely."

Then suddenly, "But how did you get here?"

THE QUESTION did not take the young man by surprise; he had been expecting it, and had gradually been formulating his answer.

So he said readily enough, "The moment that I learned of this menace to your excellency, I realized the need of getting word to you. So I broke jail—"

"Yes," interrupted the Spider. "I learned as much from my spies. Go on."

Mayhew continued, "—and made a bee-line for this volcano."

"But why didn't you go first to some spot which was within

There was a steady drone in the air as there appeared one of the strange mechanical dragon-flies which carried the priests of Ra

my occult powers to drag you here through the worluk smoke? As soon as I heard of your escape, I combed the entire city for you with my crystal globe."

"I thought of that, but dared not risk it, for fear of recapture. So, in two days' time, I reached the mountains. Not knowing any other entrance here than the shaft on the path from the excavations, I made for the sea coast, reaching the path around midnight. My first thought was to warn the guard at the diggings, but I found my way blocked by the advancing forces of the Muians. So I turned and fled before them, and barely escaped being overwhelmed by the gas and flames which Pele providentially sent to engulf them."

"Pele didn't send the flames," snarled the Spider. "I did! I, the greatest living alchemist. But continue."

"What happened after that, I do not know. I found myself lying here."

"You were picked up by one of my patrols. You nearly gave your life to save me; and quite unnecessarily, for my spy system had already warned me. So I trapped the enemy in that sunken valley, and slew them all."

"All?" echoed Mayhew, thinking of Julo and Porto and his other brave friends.

"Every man of them," growled the Spider with satisfaction. "Thus do I crush my enemies."

With superhuman effort, Mayhew forced a look of diabolic glee upon his face.

"Praise be to Pele!" he cried.

"You are tired, Tolofo," solicitously observed the Spider. "Go to your quarters. Bathe, eat, and rest. Then return, for I have urgent work for you to perform."

At his quarters, Mayhew found the faithful Moorfi in attendance. Mayhew's first question was of Eleria.

"Yes, she is here," the Negro replied, "but—praise be to Ra—the Spider has not yet sent for her. You see, Tirio has demanded her as one of the conditions of his allying himself with the Spider."

"Then they are not yet working together?"

"No. And, although the Spider has alternately threatened to throw him to Pele, and promised to share the world with him, he still holds out for Eleria."

"Does Eleria know this?"

"Yes, I believe so."

"Can you get word to her? I dare not try to see her myself."

"I think so."

"Then suggest to her the following plan of escape. Tell her who I am, and that I suggest it. She must save herself from Tirio by telling the Spider that she prefers him to the rat-faced one. This will please and flatter the Spider."

"It is rumored that she has already said as much to Tirio," interpolated Moorfi, with a grin.

Mayhew continued, "She, the peer of them all, will be the first woman ever to come to the Spider voluntarily. When she comes, and before submitting to his loathsome embraces, she must cajole him into showing her his worluk. Then let her note carefully some object in the vision which hides some near-by spot from his view. Let her leap suddenly through the smoke, and hide in that spot. It is her one chance for escape and safety."

"I understand perfectly, and will see that she does," said the Negro soberly.

Then Mayhew told him of the sad death of Julo and Porto and the rest of the expedition.

"We did not realize that the Spider possessed other powers beyond his worluk," he concluded sadly.

The huge Negro brushed a tear from his eye, then fatalistically said, "The past is behind us. It is now our problem to shape the future. I go to get word to Eleria."

"But don't tell her of Porto's death," cautioned Mayhew.

Then he bathed and ate and slept.

THE NEXT day the Spider sent for him. When he appeared before the throne and saluted, the Spider said, "Now as to your next task. I cannot come to terms with Tirio, the centurion. But there is another possible ally, who would be a thousand times more valuable, namely, Alvo, Grand High Priest of Ra. He covets my metaphysical knowledge, and especially the secret of my worluk. I need his airships. As matters now stand, I dare not leave these caves, for fear of capture. My physical infirmities put me at a great disadvantage; my distinctive appearance precludes disguise; and I cannot visit through my crystal globe, nor send my assassins through my ball of worluk smoke, to any spot which I have not visited in the flesh. So if Alvo will swap his secret of flying for my secret of worluk, I shall be able to visit many more places, and thus add them to my repertory. And I know, too, that Alvo has chafed at the supremacy of state over church. If he will ally himself with me, then together we can overthrow civil authority and make the church supreme."

"And have you proposed to the Grand High Priest this marriage of Ra and Pele?" asked Mayhew.

The Spider grinned and rubbed his skinny hands together with appreciation.

"An apt phrase," he chuckled. "The wedding of the fires of heaven to the fires of hell! No, I have not yet proposed it to Alvo. 'Tis hard to put it convincingly in writing. But you are a glib talker; so I shall send you as my ambassador."

Another chance at freedom!

"Willingly will I go," said Mayhew.

"But not in that costume or that beard," objected the Spider. "The black jersey would cause your arrest as a suspicious char-acter, and the big yellow beard would identify you as Tolofo, the escaped convict. So go to your quarters. There I shall send shears, and a razor, and a striped toga."

Mayhew saluted and left. As soon as he was out of sight, his face fell. He had to shave; it was the Spider's orders. And if he shaved, the Spider would recognize him either as Adamo Mayho or as Porto, in either of which cases his masquerade as Tolofo would be at an end.

But suddenly an idea occurred to him. Accordingly, when the shaving things arrived, he did not wholly remove his beard, but instead shaped it into the square-cut Egyptian form so preva-lent on the continent of Mu. If only this would get by with the Spider!

Then, clothed in a brilliant toga of red, white and blue—he

smiled to himself at this unconscious mark of his true nationality—he once more presented himself in the throne room.

"How do I look?" he hopefully asked.

The Spider gasped.

"Excellent! I would never know you."

"Then I'm ready to start. How do I go?"

"By worluk, but not quite yet," the Spider ominously replied, "for there is another matter which must first be disposed of. I had almost forgotten it." He clasped his hands in command. "Bring in Koko and Meeno."

Mayhew blanched. Since his return, he had forgotten that this menace still overhung him.

ATTENDANTS BROUGHT in the yellow spearman and the white slave. Mayhew, wrapped in the dignity of his toga, took his accustomed position beside the throne.

"Now, Koko," said the Spider, with oily sweetness, "you may repeat your accusations against Tolofo."

The yellow man furtively eyed the figure beside the throne.

"This is indeed Adamo Mayhew, and not Tolofo," he said, but his voice lacked the ring of positive conviction.

"Prove it!" snapped the Spider.

"My proof is Meeno, the slave."

"Meeno," said the Spider. "Is this man who stands beside me Tolofo, or is he Mayho?"

The white slave gave one terrified look at the superb figure with its striped toga and square-cut beard; then prostrated himself before the throne.

"May your excellency forgive," he whined. "It is neither. I never saw this man before."

"Oh, yes you have, Meeno," thundered Adams Mayhew. "Think. Who was it who saved you from the rush of waters? Have you no gratitude?"

"It was you," whined the slave. "I recognize the voice."

"And who am I? Tolofo or Mayho?"

He was risking everything on the fellow's terrified state of mind at finding him a favorite of the Spider.

"You are Tolofo."

"Good! And what became of Adamo Mayho?"

"He was drowned."

"And did I ever agree to help you escape, or suggest that you do so?"

"No!" The whine became a wail.

"There, your excellency," said Mayhew, turning to the throne with a shrug. "You see."

With a shriek of rage Koko, the yellow spearman, hurled his spear squarely at the Spider. It struck him in the chest and crumpled him back into a corner of the huge square throne. But—wonder of wonders—it did not penetrate.

Recovering from the blow, the Spider seized the spear and cast it contemptuously to the floor. His eyes flashed balefully.

"To Pele with both of them," he snarled. Then turning to Mayhew, and in a lighter tone, he said, "You see, I am invulnerable. I have other powers besides worluk, and the skill to loose the fumes and fires of Pele upon my enemies."

"How do you do it?" asked Mayhew, partly with real admiration, and partly from a desire to secure useful information.

The Spider leaned forward and whispered confidentially, "It's really very simple. A weapon-proof vest beneath this black jersey."

Meanwhile the two conspirators were being dragged from the room, screaming, "Mercy! Mercy, your excellency!"

Mayhew held up his hand.

"Just a moment," he said. Then, turning to the Spider, "For the spearman, no mercy; he plotted against me and tried to kill your excellency. But the slave was merely a victim and tool. He meant no harm. Spare him."

"I hope your brains are not as soft as your heart," the spider said sadly.

"Both my brains and my heart are loyal to the cause which they have espoused," Mayhew replied.

"Well said," approved the Spider, missing the hidden meaning in the words. "Very well, the man may live."

"Long life to Tolofo, and to his excellency!" cried the slave, as they led him away.

"He puts you first," remarked the Spider wryly. "And yet, why not? It was you who spared him. And now I do not feel in the mood for worluk. Send me a maiden, a plump one. And you, Tolofo, come back in an hour."

IN HIS quarters, Mayhew found Moorfi, who reported that the message had gotten through to Eleria. Then Mayhew recounted the events of the throne room.

When he reached the point where the slave had been unable to identify him either as Mayho or Tolofo, the Negro grinned and interpolated, "It must have been two other fellows, like in the story of the two men who had never been to Myax."

"We have a story like that in my own country," said the American, "only in our story the city is St. Louis."

The mention of his own country made him sad. Would he ever see it again? Had it, too, been destroyed in the same earthquake which had caused the whaling barque Alaska to vanish, and had substituted this strange and unknown Mu-dominated world for the world to which Mayhew had been accustomed?

He was still wondering about the fate of America when the Spider sent for him again. The creature was in a very business-like mood. The crystal sphere was at his side, the bowl of worluk smoking.

"You see that scene," he announced, as the smoke took shape at the waving of his hand. "This is the nearest I have ever been to the principal temple of the most high Ra. So it is there that I must start you off. Follow that path along the bank of the stream until you come to a town. It is the town of Forbosa. Inquire there for Alvo, the Grand High Priest of Ra. Give him my message and return to this spot with his answer. Mark well the spot. I will be awaiting you."

Mayhew saluted and stepped through the curtain of smoke. Then looked back.

But all signs of the Spider and his court were gone. Mayhew was standing on the green bank of a pleasant stream. He was out in the world. He was free once more. A feeling of exultation swept through his being as he stretched his arms in the warmth of the life-giving sun.

But his exalted mood was swiftly succeeded by a realization that somewhere miles away upon a skull-topped, red-marble throne, there squatted a repulsive creature, who was watching his every move, and who possessed the power to drag him back at will into the red darkness of the volcanic caves. He shuddered at the thought, and then strode resolutely forward to put as much distance as possible between himself and that loathsome form.

It was still morning, and the day was cool. There was a well defined path along the edge of the river, and walking proved to be easy. The stream was a sluggish one which wound its sinuous way, in fantastic curves and bends, through fertile meadows and around wooded hills. Tall fronded palms lined the river's banks, and at their feet were masses of great feathery ferns which spread their long arms out over the stream. Huge lacy winged dragonflies and brilliant, metallic-colored butterflies flitted about, close to the surface of the water.

AT TIMES Mayhew passed along stretches of lowlands. Here the river broadened into shallow ponds, around whose shores red and yellow and orange and blue lotus flowers dotted the thick matting of lily-pads like varicolored jewels in a setting of green gold.

At other times the river would wind between hills smothered beneath masses of impenetrable tropic jungles.

It was all serenely peaceful, serenely beautiful, and yet for Mayhew it was ominously overshadowed by the dread presence of the Spider. He could almost feel the creature's hand on his shoulder, guiding him on. He glanced apprehensively behind him.

In the dim purple distance stood the volcano; and, as Mayhew looked, the pall of smoke at its summit seemed to take definite shape; a globular black body, with eight wavy projections extending from it. Mayhew shuddered.

Shaking off this gloomy mood, so incongruous in the midst of all the lovely surroundings, he strode on.

Toward noon he began to come upon cultivated field after cultivated field, and presently reached a small village. At first he hesitated about entering this settlement, lest some one mistake him for Tolofo, the escaped convict. And, if arrested, there was now no Julo to identify and save him. But then, he reflected, this was a risk which he had to take. So he strode boldly forward into town.

Attached to the toga, which he was wearing, he found a pouch of the same material; and in this pouch there were a few coins. So he hunted out a tavern and bought himself a meal.

After ordering, he asked the waiter if this were the village of Forbosa, and also the way to the temple of the most high god. The waiter said that this was Forbosa, and directed him to the temple.

His meal over, he set out for the temple, which was not far distant.

And now, as he trudged along, he learned the identity of those huge russet-colored animals which he had seen long ago in the distance, that day in Tirio's castle. He passed many of them, both coming and going on the broad highway, and found that they were hairy elephants! Some of them were pulling large rumbling carts, while others were carrying passengers in ornate howdahs mounted on their backs.

At last he came to the temple, a stupendous structure of solid gold, or so it seemed. Its steps were of white marble surmounted by four golden figures, portraying, respectively, a man, a buffalo, an eagle, and what appeared to be a lion with oversize fangs and a short clubby tail.

Going boldly up the steps, Mayhew rapped on the temple gates. They were opened by an old man in a long yellow robe, with red swastika emblazoned upon its breast. He inquired the caller's name and business.

"Tell the Most Gracious Grand High Priest of the Flaming Ra," said Mayhew, "that my identity and my message are for his ears alone."

Such was the assurance and dignity of the caller's bearing that the temple attendant, instead of ordering him off the steps, actually ushered him into an anteroom, and then went off through resounding corridors to give the astoundingly audacious message to the Grand High Priest in person.

On his way hither, Mayhew had seriously considered proceeding to the Golden City, instead of to the temple, for he was now outside the influence of the psychic powers of the Spider. But three considerations had deterred him from this change of plans. In the first place, with Julo and Porto both dead, there would be no one to whom to turn. In the second place, it would be of utmost value to the government of Mu for him to learn and report whether an alliance was effected between the priesthood of Pele and the priesthood of Ra. And last, but not least, Eleria was still in the clutches of the Spider! So he had continued to act the emissary.

PRESENTLY THE attendant returned and reported that Alvo would see him. Accordingly he was conducted to a small and simple room, where a very old but virile man, with smooth-shaven face and yellow gown and skull cap, sat in a high-backed wooden chair behind a wooden table. The table bore ink and parchment and stylus, and was strewn with parchment manuscripts.

Shrewd eyes appraised Mayhew as he entered and gave the customary Muian salute.

"Well?" said Alvo.

"Your worship," Mayhew replied, "may this man withdraw?"

"You do not mind being searched for weapons?"

"Certainly not."

"Search him, then."

The white-bearded attendant ran his hands over Mayhew's body, removed his broadsword, then left the room.

"Be seated."

Mayhew took the proffered chair.

"And now," said Alvo, "your errand."

So Mayhew sketched, rapidly and as enticingly as he could, the proposal of the Spider for an alliance between Pele and Ra. The venerable prelate nodded from time to time, to indicate that he got some point; but, apart from this gesture, his face remained expressionless, and gave no indication as to what thoughts were going on inside his skull.

When Mayhew concluded, Alvo asked him a few brief questions, and when they had been answered, said, "This matter requires serious thought. Be our guest here until to-morrow, and then you will receive our answer."

But Mayhew shook his head, for he feared that the Spider might grow impatient awaiting his return. And so he said, "I thank your worship, but there are certain matters in Forbosa which I must attend to this afternoon. I will return to-morrow for my answer."

Alvo rang a small gold bell which sat upon the table, and the white-bearded attendant returned, gave Mayhew his sword, and showed him out.

A long, hard tramp back through Forbosa and by the side of the river remained. It was late that afternoon when he neared the spot where he was supposed to stop beside a certain tree, well-noted by him, to be sucked through the worluk haze back to the throne room of his master. But he was several hundred yards from it, around a turn in the path, when suddenly a girlish form, in flying white gown and with disheveled golden hair, dashed around the corner toward him. It was Eleria!

CHAPTER XV

THE FLAMING GOD

ON CATCHING SIGHT of the strange, square-bearded young man approaching her down the river path, Eleria halted in full flight, hesitated for an instant, and then sped on again to meet him.

"Oh," she panted, "save me! I am pursued by spider-men!"

Then she looked at him inquiringly, as though half expecting that he would scoff at her fears, for many persons in Mu were inclined to doubt the existence of the spider menace.

He laughed. "You don't recognize me, then? I'm Adams Mayhew. But quick! I must help you to escape, without implicating myself, for there is much espionage I still have to do at the court of the Spider. May I carry you?"

Tired as he was, she was probably far more tired.

She hesitated for a moment, then blushed and nodded. So Mayhew swung her light body into his strong arms and ran back toward Forbosa with her, along the river path. He realized, however, that the assassins of the Spider were probably gaining on them.

Accordingly, when presently they reached a fork in the road, he lowered her gently to the ground and said, "Here, quick, into that clump of bushes. Any bits of your dress which may show through the leaves will be mistaken for its white flowers. I will go back and try to head the spearmen off. If I succeed, you lie here for about an hour and then push on to Forbosa. If I fail, I shall try to divide the party at this bush. Follow me, if I go down one trail alone. Good-by, and good luck."

And he strode off to meet the oncoming assassins. Only a few paces and they were upon him, three of them. If he had been a strange Muian gentleman, things would have gone hard with him; another body would have been found, floating in a stream, with the mark of the Spider pinned to its breast by a dagger. Fortunately one of the men had seen him in the throne-room in his new beard and attire, so this man hailed him as an ally, and inquired excitedly if he had seen Eleria.

"Why no!" exclaimed Mayhew, showing a perturbation which he really felt. "What do you mean?"

"His excellency was waiting for your return, with her in his arms," explained the spearman, "when suddenly she stood up, jumped through the screen of worluk smoke, and fled. His excellency was so upset by this that the ball of smoke wavered and broke. He had to send for a new bowl of powder, and by the time he got it going again the girl was out of sight. But he had been watching her all the time in his crystal globe, and we had been summoned and were standing in readiness. As soon as the new smoke formed he sent us through. She went along this path, he said."

"Quick, then, let us catch her!" directed Mayhew. "It is quite a distance to town, and she will tire long before she reaches it."

"But how can it be you did not see her? That is, unless she left the path."

"I doubt if she left the path; she would have been too frightened and excited to do anything but flee. However, just a few steps from here there is a fork. She must have gone down the other branch from the one I was on. One of you," pointing to the one he knew, "go back to his excellency. Report to him that I gave his message to the person to whom it was directed, that I am spending the night in Forbosa, and that I have the appointment for tomorrow noon to receive my answer. Also report what we are doing about this search. The rest of us will go on to the fork, and there divide."

"Very well, sir," replied the spearman.

Saluting, he turned and went back along the path.

"Come on!" said Mayhew to the other two.

A few paces on they reached the parting of the ways.

Mayhew said, "I came down the right-hand path, so she must have gone down the left, or I would have met her. You two go down the left-hand path as fast as you can run. If she has gone that way, you can undoubtedly catch her. I will take the right-hand path on the chance that she may have eluded me on that route. If I catch her I will drag her back. If not I will put up for the night at the inn. Don't venture too near the town. Now—run!"

THEY RAN. So did Mayhew, down the other path of the fork. But as soon as they were out of sight, he stopped and waited. Soon Eleria hurried up to him. Together they went on to the town, she running and being carried by turns.

They reached the town-without mishap and without meeting any one. On the outskirts, Mayhew gave the girl some of his money, and they entered town separately, lest they be seen by spies of the Spider. Separately they put up at the inn. Eleria sent out for a garment more conventional than the filmy white gown in which she had fled. Both freshened themselves up, and then met surreptitiously in Eleria's room.

First she detailed how she had followed out the suggestions which he had sent her through Moorfi.

"The only snag," she said, "was the matter of clothes. Of course, if I had to, I could have worn that awful harem costume."

She blushed prettily, and Mayhew coughed embarrassedly at a recollection of those yellow girls crawling hypnotized into the arms of the Spider.

"But," she continued, "how could I run through the country in that deshabille? Imagine my entering Forbosa with nothing on!"

She laughed gayly, the humor of the situation overcoming her embarrassment.

"And so," she went on, "I persuaded that fatuous old fool of a hunchback to clothe me in a costume more fitting to the dignity of an empress, than to the physical seductiveness of a harem. You know, the Spider has actually asked me to marry him."

Mayhew expressed horror.

"It's scarcely any better than to be one of his concubines," he asserted indignantly.

"Except that it's more complimentary," she pouted.

"I don't believe you really mean that," he said.

"Forgive me for being facetious," she replied, sobering. "You have risked your life to save mine, which is more than I deserve after treating you the way I did back there in the Golden City."

"I would gladly do anything for you," he blurted out; then to cover up his confusion, he went hurriedly on to say, "and the way you treated me was perfectly all right, you know, for you thought that I was some one else."

At this mention of "some one else," he suddenly remembered that the disagreeable task lay ahead of him of breaking the news to her of the death of Porto. He coughed, and hesitated.

Noticing his perturbation, she asked, "What is the matter?"

"Oh, nothing. Nothing," he said hurriedly. "What do you plan to do next? You can't stay in Forbosa even overnight. There will be spies here, searching."

"Why, I suppose," she mused aloud, "that I shall send a message to Julo, and then start at once for the Golden City. There is probably a night-elephant running between here and there."

Mayhew looked sadly upon her, and strove to think of adequate words by which to convey the news of Julo's death.

Finally he merely blurted it out, and then recounted to her the sad story of the ill-fated expedition.

When he finished she burst into tears.

"You do not need to tell me the rest," she said. "For I know. I can feel it. If there was dangerous patriotic adventure to be had, my Porto would have been in it. And now he's dead, along with the rest. Oh, to think that I called him a coward! And even after I learned that he had not been a coward, I flirted with Tirio, just to annoy Porto. And now Porto's gone, gone without knowing that I love him. May Ra forgive me!"

SHE FLUNG her arms around Adams Mayhew's neck, and sobbed upon his shoulder.

It was exquisite pleasure to have her slender arms about him, and her dear head nestling on his shoulder. And he was truly sympathetic with her grief. But the cause of it gave him many a twinge of jealousy.

At last she raised her head and stifled her sobs. Firmly setting her pointed chin, she tried to stiffen her still quivering lips.

"I must go now," she said. "Come and see me the next time you are in the Golden City." Then, with a sudden thought: "Come with me now. Why can't you come with me now?"

He was sadly torn between love and duty.

"There's nothing I would like better," he said. "But I owe it to Julo's memory—and to Porto's too—to carry on the fight which they started. There is much still to be learned of the Spider's plans and powers, and I mean to do it. Until he is disposed of, none of us is safe."

"Why not kill him and be done with it? Haven't you had the opportunity?"

"I've thought of that," said he soberly, "but, in the first place, he is invulnerable, or nearly so. And, in the second place, I am convinced that he has a group of other master minds in the background, ready to take over, if anything should occur to him. He is too clever to overlook the need for that."

Then Mayhew told the girl all that he knew of the Spider's powers and plans, culminating in his proposed alliance with the priests of Ra.

"After tomorrow's conference," he said, "I shall send a note to you. It will say merely 'yes' or 'no.' Thus will I inform you whether or not the alliance has been effected. Then will you please go to the authorities and tell them all you know. I shall return to the Spider to learn more. If I ever escape him, I shall come to see you."

To his surprise, she flung her arms once more around his neck, sobbing out, "Don't go! I don't want you to go. I've lost Julo, and Porto, and every one I know; and I don't want to lose you too. You're all I have left in the world, except an old uncle. I don't want you to die. Come back with me to the Golden City!"

Gently he disengaged her.

"Dearest," he said, "I must go. You would despise me if I quit the job now. Julo and Porto must be avenged. The faithful Moorfi, who helped to save you, is counting on my return. I must go back."

She dried her tears. He kissed her tenderly.

"Good-by, dear," he said. "Go downstairs now, and find out about the night-elephant."

He kissed her again, while she clung pitifully to him. Then he left the room and did not see her again before her departure.

That evening, in the main room of the inn, he kept his ears open for news of any untoward occurrences in the vicinity, but heard of none. He slept soundly in his room—how much better the fresh air of Forbosa than the sulphur-tainted fumes of the caves of Pele—and left the next morning, shortly before noon, for the temple of Ra.

His heart sang as he walked along, for his thoughts were of the lovely Eleria.

AT THE temple he was admitted without delay and was led at once to the plain small office of Alvo, the unpretentious supreme potentate of the prevailing religion of the entire Empire of the Sun. As he entered; he inadvertently gave the Roman salute of Pele, instead of the triangular gesture of Ra, and the prelate frowned.

But quickly dissembling his displeasure, he said, "I suppose you have come for our answer to your master, the Spider."

"Yes," said Mayhew.

"Very well. You shall have it, all in due time." Not one muscle of that poker-face gave the least inkling what the answer was to be. "But first may I be permitted to do you the courtesy of showing you through our beautiful temple? You have never been here before?"

Mayhew shook his head.

"Oh, of course," agreed the prelate, and there was just the faintest tinge of scorn in his suave old voice. "A worshiper of Pele would not be apt to be familiar with the temples of Ra."

"I worship neither Pele nor Ra," said Mayhew without thinking; then bit his lip.

But apparently no harm was done, for the high priest replied, "Ah, an atheist then. But even so, you appear to be a cultivated gentleman, who can appreciate good architecture."

Impatient as Mayhew was to learn the result of his embassy, he could not but politely accept the honor.

So the priest rang for another old man of nearly his own age and appearance, and together they conducted their guest through the temple. From the study of the high priest they took him down a long corridor lined with the cells where dwelt the lesser priests and attendants. Several of these cells they showed him; all were Spartan in their simplicity and military in their neatness.

But the huge hall of worship was quite different. Never, since his arrival on the island of Mu, had Adams Mayhew seen so much gold. Every inch of the white marble walls was encrusted with ingeniously carved gold fretwork. Like the temple which he had visited in the Golden City, this room was built in the form of an amphitheater, surrounded with tiers of marble seats; and above the seats a canopy of fluted gold, supported by spiral gold pillars. Beyond the canopy, this room, like the other, had no roof, being completely open to the sky. It was one of the "transparent temples," for which Mu was noted. He complimented the two old priests on its stupendous beauty!

"You have seen nothing yet!" they said, flashing a glance at one another. "For now, as a special tribute of hospitality, we shall show you the holy of holies, a sight which is vouchsafed to few, even of the priesthood."

Murmuring his unworthiness of this great honor, and really anxious to receive his answer and be on his way, Mayhew followed them through a small door beneath one of the sections of seats, and down a long dark corridor, at the end of which one of the priests fumbled with a key in a lock.

At last a door swung open, admitting them to a small dim room. At first, all that Mayhew could make out was a single narrow shaft of bright sunlight, slanting down to the floor from a small round hole in the ceiling. All else was dark and indistinct by contrast.

Then, as his eyes became used to the peculiar combination of brilliance and gloom, he noticed in the exact center of the chamber a gray stone about five feet long, four feet high, and two feet thick, with a slightly rounded top. This stone looked as though it once had been white, but now it was streaked and stained and aged to a mottled gray—gray mottled with brown. On the side nearest him there hung a ring and two straps of gold.

"The altar of the Most High Ra," said Alvo. "Step nearer, favored one, and see a sight which few see."

Fascinated, Mayhew stepped forward. He arrived at the stone and leaned over to inspect it. Suddenly, with a precision which evidenced long practice, the two old men leaped upon him, seized his shoulders, swung him around, and bent him backward across the stone. In an instant, rings far down each side of the stone were snapped about his wrists, and one golden strap was bound across his neck, the other across his hips.

His two captors stepped back and gloated over him. Then one of them reached into a niche in the wall and brought forth a long slim knife.

"Thus die those who dare oppose the religion of the one true god," he hissed.

CHAPTER XVI

HUMAN SACRIFICE

MAYHEW STRAINED AND wrenched at his bonds, but they would not give an inch. He desisted.

"I have not opposed your god," he replied.

"You came to us as the emissary of Pele, did you not?"

"Yes, but—"

"Then for that you must die."

In desperation, Adams Mayhew decided to tell the truth as to his identity. Surely these priests, who had thus repulsed the offers of the Spider, could be trusted to keep his secret.

"I am a spy, a government spy," he blurted out. "Captured by the Spider, I changed places with one of his henchmen who died. I have won his confidence. I pass freely in and out of his domain, and have given much valuable information to the authorities. I came here yesterday and today—sent by the Spider, it is true— but for the real purpose of sounding you out."

"An insult!" shouted the lesser priest. "An insult which shall be effaced by your death!"

But Alvo stopped him with, "Peace! Desist! We should be calmly and serenely above all insult, in reliance on the knowledge that the great Ra, who sees all and knows all, has faith in us. But," turning to the victim on the altar, "it does interest us to learn if the government shares your suspicions of us."

"Certainly not," Mayhew hastened to aver. "It was entirely my own idea."

Alvo appeared much relieved.

"The government will not thank you for having meddled in our affairs," he said dryly. "What is your name, infidel?"

Mayhew had not even introduced himself as Tolofo, for fear of being turned over to the authorities as an escaped convict. Now, for a moment he hesitated. He had three names to choose from. The name "Tolofo" might still get him into trouble, and thus prevent him from returning to spy upon the Spider, and rescue the faithful Moorfi. The name "Adamo Mayho" would doubtless mean nothing to them. Hence he selected the third available name.

"I am Porto," he said, "of the Golden City."

Both men looked at him carefully.

"He does resemble Porto," admitted the lesser priest. "I have had the man pointed out to me. But Porto wore no beard."

"I have only recently grown it."

To the other priest Alvo said, "There is yet time to check up on this."

So the other left on a waddling run. During his absence, Mayhew pleaded with Alvo, but the latter turned a deaf ear to his pleas.

At last the lesser prelate returned with an ominous gleam in his eye, and reported, "I heliographed to our temple in the Golden City, and they state that Porto is there."

"But that is impossible!" Mayhew blurted out, taken completely off his guard by the astounding news. "Porto can't be there. He died in the attack on the stronghold of the Spider."

"So!" hissed Alvo. "Then you are an impostor, by your own admission. Thus die the enemies of Ra!"

"But I tell you, I *am* a government spy," pleaded Mayhew frantically. "If you kill me, you're hurting the cause of Ra; not helping it. I'm Adamo Mayho, as they call me in the Golden City.

"I'm the double of Porto, and I took his name, thinking that he was dead, and that you would be more likely to know of him than of me."

Swords out, they
pierced through the line

"Somehow his words have the ring of truth in them," mused the high priest. "But he is an atheist."

"I'm not an atheist," objected Mayhew. "I worship Ra, but by another name."

"Everything about you seems to masquerade under other names," snapped Alvo dryly. "But enough of this nonsense. The time for the execution has arrived."

SEEING THAT there was no further hope, Mayhew stopped

his pleas and clenched his jaw; resolving that if he must die, he would at least die like a man, instead of a cringing coward.

"Go ahead and strike!" he challenged them.

"Not yet," replied the lesser priest, grinning ghoulishly, or so Mayhew imagined. "We do not strike until the eye of Ra falls upon your left breast. Then we snatch out your living heart, and offer it, still beating, unto our god."

The "eye of Ra" was quite evidently the shaft of brilliant sunlight, shining down through the small orifice in the ceiling of this dungeon, and by now almost touching the right side of the victim. Mayhew twisted his head as far to the right as the golden strap across his neck would permit, and observed the shaft of light.

Its approach was uncannily steady. On and on came the golden ray of death; while Alvo, the Grand High Priest of Ra, stood expectantly at the head of the altar, the sharp sacrificial knife hanging poised in his upraised hand; and the other old priest, standing at the foot of the altar, began to intone "the death chant of the flaming god."

"O, Ra," he sang, "shine thy approval on this offering which we bring to thee. Touch his heart with thy shaft of gold, so that we may know that thou hast chosen him for the sacrifice."

The chant droned on and on. The sunbeam approached the altar and bathed the side of the stone and the right arm of Adams Mayhew. He could feel its warmth on his elbow. Then it passed over the edge of the altar and shone upon the right side of his chest.

Fascinated, he followed it with his eyes, then shifted his gaze to the sharp knife which hung poised above his diaphragm. He no longer needed to watch the ray of light, for he could feel the progress of its warmth across his body. So he watched the knife, knowing that when the ray passed to a position above his heart, his chest would be ripped open with one swift stroke, and his still beating heart would be plucked out. What happened after that would no longer concern him.

As the ray of death traversed his breast-bone, he tensed his muscles and steeled his nerves to meet the end. The chant ceased. There came an ominous pause. Then the knife began its descent.

Mayhew gasped, and shut his eyes to blot out the sight. A sudden feeling of coolness swept, across his chest. Was this the way the fatal knife-thrust felt? And could it be that he still lived to feel it?

He waited for the outplucking of his heart, but it did not come. He heard an exclamation of disgust from one of the priests. Then he reopened his eyes. The room was in darkness. There was no shaft of light. And through the opening in the ceiling, the sky showed gray, not blue. A cloud was passing across the face of Ra, the sun.

CHAPTER XVII

THE KNIFE

AT LENGTH THE sky, as seen through the tiny aperture in the roof of the crypt, turned from gray to blue again. The shaft of sunlight beat down once more through the opening. The high priest leaned forward again with his sacrificial dagger eagerly poised above the breast of Adams Mayhew.

But it was too late. The time for the sacrifice had passed, for the shaft of light had gone beyond the breast of the intended victim, and would not shine upon the blood-stained altar again until high noon of another day.

"Ra blast him to Pele!" snarled the lesser of the two priests.

"Silence!" exclaimed Alvo reprovingly. "Such language in the holy temple is most unseemly!"

"Why not kill him even now?" urged the other. "No man will ever know but what we struck while the light was upon him."

"No man would know," mildly replied the high priest. "But Ra would know, and it would be on our consciences forever. Ra himself has refused to accept our sacrifice, so we must await another day."

"Shall we leave him here, or shall we remove him; and if so, just how?"

"That does present a difficulty," mused Alvo. "We are two old and feeble men. If we release him, he might destroy us. But on the other hand we cannot permit any lesser priests and temple attendants to enter this holy of holies, for the purpose of guarding us. And if we leave him here for twenty-four hours, he may

141

perish of the strain, or at least become so weakened that his heart will not be beating strongly as we pluck it out on the morrow. We are indeed in a quandary."

This conversation was being carried on in utter disregard of the presence of Adams Mayhew, as though he were a mere bit of furniture or a lower animal. He decided that it was time for him to take a part in the conversation.

So he interposed, "As proof of my innocence and good faith, O Alvo, I will give you my word of honor that, if you release me, I will attempt no violence, nor will I try to escape until you have gotten me out of here and have placed me in the hands of competent guards."

"The word of a heretic is meaningless, Alvo," warned the lesser priest.

But Alvo replied, "Even so, I am inclined to believe him, at least this much. Do you therefore unshackle him, while I go to summon husky guards to await just outside the entrance to the tunnel which leads from the amphitheater to this spot."

He placed the sacrificial knife back in its niche and departed. The door clanged shut behind him. The other priest leaned over the altar and gloated at Adams Mayhew. Then he walked to the niche, picked up the sacrificial knife, and returned to the altar.

HIS EYES gleamed exultantly and evilly as he hissed, "And now, heretic, we are alone together. No one but you and I can know what shall now occur within this crypt. I shall slice your wrists in such a way as to make it appear that you chafed them raw against your manacles. Then I shall run and tell Alvo that you became so violent that I dared not loosen you. No one but you and I will know the truth, and you shall be dead, wandering, a lost soul, through the realms of Pele."

Seeking to appeal to the man's superstition, Mayhew exclaimed, "But Ra will know. Ra sees everything."

The priest shook his head and grinned toothlessly.

"Even Ra will not know," he asserted, "for Ra hides his head today."

It was true; the sky again showed leaden gray through the hole in the top of the crypt.

Still gloating, the priest cautiously took hold of one of Mayhew's wrists and studied it to find a place where his slashings would most plausibly resemble the chafing of the manacles. Mayhew strained to snatch it free, but its fetters held it motionless. Carefully the priest began to saw.

But at that instant Mayhew suddenly remembered that his legs were free. His neck was strapped to the top of the altar and his wrists to its sides, but his feet and legs were free. The priest was preoccupied with his delicate task.

So Mayhew reared his legs into the air and flung his knees around the neck of the old man. Then he squeezed with all the force of his strong young thighs. The attack was so unexpected that the priest dropped the knife, which would have been a most efficient means of defense against even these tactics. He tried to scream, but his wind was completely cut off by the strong legs of his intended victim.

Mayhew squeezed and squeezed, until the body of the priest slumped and went limp. Yet still he continued to squeeze, until he himself was exhausted. Then he lay back on the altar and let the body slide to the floor.

His enemy was dead. But, in the reaction which followed his fatiguing efforts, he felt nothing but supreme despair, for he had killed a priest of Ra within the holy of holies, and thereby had undoubtedly sealed his own doom irrevocably. Limp and tired, he awaited his fate.

ALVO RETURNED, flung open the door, gasped at the sight of his dead subordinate, and then transfixed the man on the altar with a penetrating glance of horror and reproach.

"You broke your word of honor, pledged by the holy name of Ra," he said. "And for that you shall most assuredly die."

"Alvo," asserted Mayhew in a level tone, "I killed in self defense. This priest of yours—you will remember how eager he was to profane the altar of the flaming god by killing me at other than the appointed hour. When you left, he tried to do it. See, the holy dagger is no longer in its niche, but lies on the floor there, where he dropped it, when I defended myself against his cowardly attack. He—"

"Enough," snapped Alvo, his eyes blazing. "Doubtless he carried the dagger merely as a defense against the violence which he expected—quite rightly, as it now turns out—from a false-swearing heretic such as you."

"But I did not break my oath," pleaded Mayhew. "I swore to be peaceful if and when released; and he refused to release me."

"A mere quibble," sneered Alvo contemptuously, "for he was about to release you. But I will hear no more. Lie there and await your fate."

Then, picking up the body, he staggered with it from the crypt. Mayhew could hear him shout, as he passed down the corridor, "Come hither, guards, and help me bear this body to the amphitheater, where we shall pray to Ra to restore life to this, his faithful servant."

Mayhew sniffed grimly. Circumstantial evidence, all against him. And yet he could hardly blame the high priest.

About an hour later Alvo returned, with a very sad and enigmatical expression on his finely chiseled old face.

"Ra has refused to revive your victim," he said. "The flaming god still averts his face. Perhaps there may be some truth to your account of what happened here in my absence. But I can afford to take no further chances with you. Here you must lie until noon tomorrow. Then, at high noon, let Ra judge between you and me."

He departed. For a time, Mayhew slept. That wasn't so bad. But finally he could sleep no more. He was able to exercise the lower part of his body, but the cramped position of his arms and neck became excruciating.

Morning came, and his senses cleared, though his neck and arms were numb, and his throat was parched and dry. Pink fleecy sky showed through the hole in the ceiling, but this speedily changed to gray. Darker and darker gray.

At this sight, Mayhew took heart. Perhaps Ra would again avert his face, and spare the victim for another twenty-four hours. But could he stand this ordeal for that additional length of time? In the end, there must eventually come a clear and unclouded noon. And then the knife!

He shuddered. Then, with determination, he began to flex and unflex his almost nerveless fingers. He lifted and twisted each shoulder. He swung his head slowly from side to side. He brought into play every one of his cramped muscles, and gradually the blood flooded back into them, and he was thoroughly alive again, alive from head to toe.

But, as the morning dragged wearily on, his hope began to fade. The sky, as seen through the small opening above him, changed to lighter gray, then white. Occasional rifts of blue appeared. And then the shaft of sunlight entered, and made a spot of light on one of the walls. That spot began to descend. It reached the floor, and crept ominously toward the altar. Footsteps sounded in the corridor outside, and Alvo entered with another priest, a young one this time.

CHAPTER XVIII

THE DEAD RETURN

"**THIS YOUNG FELLOW** owes his promotion to you," the high priest announced with a grim smile. "For the exigencies of the occasion have demanded that I pass him over the heads of many of his seniors, in order that the vicar of Ra on earth may be protected against any repetition of your violence."

"Alvo," Mayhew levelly replied, "it astounds me that such an evidently intelligent person as you should not be blessed by Ra with the knowledge that, in attempting to strike at the Spider through putting to death a supposed emissary of his, you are in reality playing into his hands by doing away with the one man in all Mu who is in a position to thwart him."

"Enough of these blasphemies!" shouted the high priest with flashing eyes. "Do not let the name of Ra cross your impious lips again. The service proceeds."

He snatched the knife from its niche, and took up his position by the side of the altar. The young priest stood at the altar's foot and began the death-chant of Ra. It was evidently quite new to him, and he sang it haltingly. But what did that matter! The sky was clear above, the "eye of Ra" approached with relentless precision, and the sacrificial blade was in steady and experienced hands.

A shout was heard in the corridor outside. "Alvo, a message! A message of most vital import!"

With a shrug of annoyance the high priest studied for a moment the position of the beam of light.

"There is yet time," he announced. "Suspend the chant. I go, but I shall return."

Then, laying the knife upon the floor, he sped from the room. Mayhew's tensed body relaxed and he sighed heavily. Then he had an idea.

"Say, old fellow," he addressed the young priest. "You owe your job to me. If you are grateful—no, I won't put it on that ground. If you are alive to the responsibilities of your new position as assistant vicar of Ra, can't you persuade Alvo to hold up this execution until he investigates the truth of what I've been saying? It would be a terrible tragedy to help the Spider by killing the one loyal Muian who has access to the secrets of that fiend of Pele."

"It might be done," the young priest thoughtfully replied. "Certainly if you are telling the truth, your death would be on our consciences forever. And yet—let Ra decide! He knows all things. If you are innocent, he will withhold his eye."

"Look here," said Mayhew. "Send for Marta, the widow of the magistrate Julo. She can identify me. She knows how I helped her husband in his plans against the Spider."

"Yes, I've heard about that. You led him and many other brave men into an ambush, from which the survivors have just returned. Doubtless Marta will thank you for *that!* We learned all about it by heliograph early yesterday afternoon. Your identity was quite well established, before Ra finally hid his face for good."

Mayhew groaned. Every fact on which he had depended for exoneration seemed to be turned against him. The priests now knew that he had been telling the truth as to who he was, and yet they still believed that he deserved to die.

AT THIS instant Alvo bustled in again. The young priest resumed the chant of death.

But Alvo interrupted with, "No. No! There is to be no sacrifice. Release the prisoner."

Mayhew slumped, and his senses reeled with relief.

As the two priests fumbled with his bonds, he shook himself again and weakly inquired, "What has happened?"

"Ra be praised that the message came through in time," said Alvo devoutly. "But then it was Ra's own self that delivered the message. Ever since Ra hid his face yesterday afternoon, the temple in the Golden City has been trying to get word to us that you are indeed a loyal friend of the government, and an enemy of the Spider."

Tenderly they helped him from the altar and led him out of the room of death. As they all passed out of the tunnel into the amphitheater a surprising sight met Mayhew's eyes; Porto, standing with outstretched hands of greeting.

"But," Mayhew exclaimed, "the Spider said that every man of the expedition perished."

"He may have thought so," replied Porto. "What happened was that we advanced in two bodies. Only the smaller body, which served as an advance guard, was trapped. The rest of us fled back to the ships, and returned to the Golden City for reenforcements. From now on we fight in the open. All Mu is being aroused to the necessity of destroying the Spider."

"And Eleria—"

"Arrived safely at home yesterday morning. She is being carefully guarded."

"I'll wager that you had considerable to do with saving my life just now."

"I did, but it was a close shave. The temple in the city sent out inquiries as to whether I was there or here. Word of this inquiry reached me a few hours later. At once I sensed that you must be the cause. By the time I learned that you were to be executed as an impostor it was evening, and so we could not send a heliograph message. Leaving word that the message must be gotten through with the first clear sky, I set out for here. I traveled all night. My elephant proved balky and delayed me. I was desperate. I arrived here just now, to find that the message had gotten through, and that you were saved."

At this point the high priest interrupted to say sententiously: "Glory be to Ra, who delivered the message, before he smiled upon the sacrifice."

"Didn't I say that it could be safely left to Ra?" added the young priest.

MAYHEW AND Porto were served a meal in the personal apartment of the high priest. The latter withdrew in response to a summons from an attendant.

"I could be very happy," Mayhew asserted, "if Moorfi were free, and if Julo hadn't been killed."

"What's this?" said a genial voice from the doorway. "Lamenting my death, Adamo Mayho?"

And Julo himself stepped into the room, accompanied by the high priest.

"I thought I told you!" exclaimed Porto. "Julo was with the party that did not fall into the web of the Spider."

It was a glad reunion. After the greetings were over Mayhew related in detail all that had occurred since their last meeting, and all that he had learned about the Spider.

"Come back with us to the city," begged Julo. "You have risked enough for the cause. Eleria and we are now safe. Fight in our army if you wish, but do not again thrust yourself between the Spider's jaws."

"I must," said Mayhew soberly. "Moorfi is still in the caves of Pele, and I cannot desert him. Furthermore, it is important that we learn how the attempted alliance with Tirio and his confederates is working out. And also what other secrets the Spider must have up his sleeve."

"I guess you are right," assented Julo thoughtfully, "but I hate to have you go. You are almost a son to me. And I owe you my life at least once. Yes, you had better go. And there is one thing which I wish you to particularly try to learn. What is the purpose of those extensive excavations, on which the Spider is so assiduously working? I cannot even guess, and yet I feel certain that they constitute the worst menace that has ever confronted this continent; far more of a menace than merely the Spider himself."

So that afternoon Mayhew went back through Forbosa to a certain tree by the bank of the lotus-strewn stream, and waited.

He waited for some time, for evidently the Spider was not expecting him. But at last he saw the red haze which he had learned to know so well, and passed through the screen of worluk into the cave of the Spider. Once more he stood before his master.

The Spider's narrowed and penetrating eyes were upon him, seeming to read his very thoughts.

"Where have you been all this time? And why did you delay in returning?" hissed the creature.

"Perhaps your excellency would first care to know the results of my mission," Mayhew coolly replied.

"Tolofo," said the Spider with one of his characteristic rapid shifts of mood, "one thing that I like about you is the way that you stand up to me, instead of cringing before me like all these cattle. Yes, you may tell me about your mission, although I can see from the expression on your face that it was not successful."

"No, your excellency," Mayhew replied, in as regretful a tone as he could muster. "Not only was it unsuccessful for you, but it was almost fatal to me. In revenge for what they considered was an insult to their god, the priests strapped me to their sacrificial altar for twenty-four hours. But twice Ra declined the sacrifice by hiding his face at exactly the appointed hour, and so the superstitious fools let me go. But it was a narrow escape."

"I wonder," mused the Spider softly, but with an intent though covert glance at Mayhew, "if Ra himself really intervened to save you."

"Who knows?" the young man replied with a shrug. "Perhaps Pele sent a wisp of smoke to hide her rival's face."

The answer seemed to satisfy the Spider.

MAYHEW, SEEKING information, continued, "But, although

the priesthood refused to ally themselves with you, how about Tirio? His secret anti-government organization has more men and more influential men than the priesthood. Has he yet assented to an alliance?"

"He has," the hunchback scientist replied. "The escape of Eleria was really fortunate, for it removed the only obstacle to my reaching an agreement with Tirio. And—although he doesn't know this—I intend to have Eleria for myself as soon as I rule the world. Tirio's price for the alliance is that he is to be the chief magistrate of the Golden City. He thinks thereby to secure both power and the girl. But I can plan at least one lap ahead of him."

"I am sure your excellency can," breathed the American.

"And now," the Spider continued, "I shall send for Tirio. Somehow he seems to feel that you harbor a hatred for him, because of his complicity in your original imprisonment."

"Not at all," said Mayhew. "Far be it from me to let that stand between me and a loyal ally of your excellency."

So Tirio was sent for. On his entry he looked at Mayhew most carefully. This was the first time that he had seen the supposed Tolofo in a toga, rather than a black jersey and tights; or since his bushy blond beard had been reduced to small square-cut Egyptian form. A gradual dawning of recognition spread over Tirio's features.

"Your excellency," he cried, "this is not Tolofo. It is either Porto or Adamo Mayho. I know not which, for they are as alike as twins."

"Tirio," the American replied undisturbed, "is this your attempted revenge on Tolofo for having captured you and brought you here? A very weak attempt, I should say. And besides, you ought to be grateful, rather than resentful, that I was the means of this meeting. Few men, other than members of your order, have had the honor of seeing the face of his excellency, and continuing to live."

"Yes, Tirio," added the Spider, but he was intently studying Mayhew as he spoke. "And men have been thrown to Pele quite recently for doubting the identity of this loyal supporter of mine."

Tirio saw that he was in a corner; and, with the bravery of a cornered rat, he blurted out, "Who killed Tolofo, and took his place as overseer? Who leaped through the screen of worluk, to save the life of your enemy Julo, whom your assassins were about to kill? Who gave away your secrets, and led the expedition to attack you? Who got word to Eleria how to escape? Who harbored her when she had fled you? Who persuaded the high priest of Ra to spurn your most fair offer of alliance? And who has now boldly come back to plot against us? Oh, you have been blind, your excellency!"

It was a perfect indictment. Mayhew blanched, in spite of his self control.

And the Spider, seeing this, cried, "You are right, Tirio. I *have* been blind. Ho, guards! Seize the false Tolofo! Pele shall be fed today."

CHAPTER XIX

A HUNCHBACKED SAMSON

AS THE SPEARMEN sprang to seize him, Mayhew drew his sword and leaped at the Spider. It was a most unwise move, for it destroyed his last chance of convincing the Spider that he was Tolofo. And it enabled the rat-faced Tirio to solidify himself with the monarch of the underworld, by stepping nimbly forward and with his own sword parrying Mayhew's blow.

The Spider was quivering with rage and his taloned fingers were gripping the arms of the throne.

"Let there be no delay," he shrieked. "Take him to the eternal fires at once. And bring my chair-car, so that I may accompany him, and witness, with my own eyes, his destruction."

"May I make a suggestion, your excellency?" inquired Tirio in a gloating voice. "The Negro attendant of this Mayho, or Porto, or Tolofo, or whoever he is, was formerly of the house of Julo, your enemy.

"Doubtless therefore the Negro is also implicated in the conspiracy against you. May I suggest that he too goes to feed the eternal fires?"

The Spider rubbed his hands with evil glee as he exclaimed:

"In truth, Pele shall feast well today. Yes, Tirio, by all means send for the Negro, Moorfi."

Mayhew was hustled along, through caves and subterranean passages, to the vaulted cavern which held the surging pit of molten lava. Moorfi, bound hand and foot, joined them on the way. The huge Negro refused to walk, even to the accompani-

ment of prodding spear-points, so the spider-men were forced
to carry him.

As he joined the group he sung out jovially to Mayhew,
"Master, you haven't the right idea at all. They're making *you*
walk, and here *I* am, riding. It reminds me of the story of the two
black men who were stealing chickens. Did you ever hear it?"

But Mayhew was in no mood for ribald stories.

"Keep your eyes open, Moorfi," said he tensely. "We may yet
get a chance to fight."

The Spider followed them in a chair, slung on two poles; and
by his side walked the odious Tirio.

At the cave of Pele, the Spider directed the attention of his
new ally to the surging lava.

"These are the eternal fires," he said. "And since the grand
high priest spurns my offer of a marriage between Ra and Pele,
I am contemplating another marriage."

Mayhew thought that the creature was referring to a marriage
between his stunted self and the beautiful Eleria; but not so,
for the Spider continued, "This other marriage, which I have
planned for the fire-goddess, is with the god of Ocean. That is
why I have dug a canal from the sea to here. My canal is nearly
completed. At any moment now I can, at will, flood the sea-
water into this very pit."

MAYHEW PRICKED up his ears and listened intently.

"But would that not be dangerous?" asked Tirio in a voice
which shook with concern.

"Quite so," the Spider suavely replied, "for it would destroy
the entire world."

"But—your excellency," Tirio stammered.

"Oh, I shan't do it," the Spider continued. Tirio brightened
perceptibly. "Except as a last resort."

Tirio's face fell again, as he asked, "And what do you mean
'as a last resort'?"

"If I cannot rule the world, I intend that there shall remain

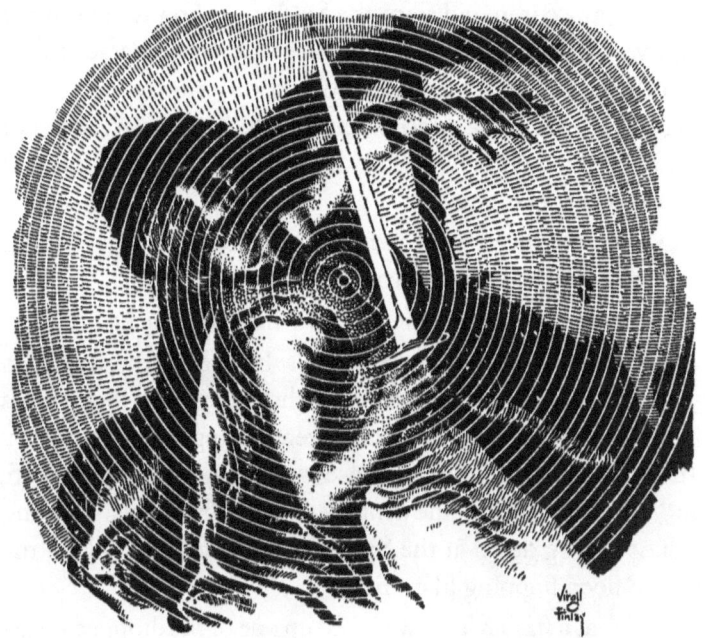

With his sword drawn to defy the Spider, Mayhew
felt a surge of disembodied force which seemed to
strike against him and he staggered backward

no world for any one else to rule. This should prove an added cement to our alliance, for now you realize that unless your and my combined forces succeed in conquering Mu, then you and I will die along with all the rest. But enough of all this talk, for I am sick of talk, and demand action. Let the execution proceed!"

Mayhew edged closer to his faithful Negro, and whispered in his ear, "Did you catch all that about letting the sea into the volcano? Well, remember it in all its details. One of us has just got to get out of here, and take word of this to Julo."

"I wouldn't mind doing that at all," Moorfi replied with a rather sickly grin on his round black face, "but it doesn't look very likely at just this moment. It reminds me of the story—"

But one of the yellow spearmen slapped him across the mouth, and he desisted.

Then, at a command from the Spider, the bonds of both the captives were untied, a ring of spear-points encompassed them, and they were simultaneously pushed very slowly toward the edge of the seething inferno. They could hear the chuckles of the mad monarch as he rubbed his skinny hands together, and gloated over their fate.

Mayhew glanced back and Tirio sang out to him, "A fitting end to that fight at the wharves."

"So that still rankles, does it?" Mayhew shot back at him.

At that moment the spearmen who were prodding him suddenly turned and ran, several of them dropping their spears in their flight. All the attendants were fleeing from the cavern. There remained but two of those who were prodding Moorfi, and even these were showing hesitancy. Tirio was standing aghast staring down at the Spider, who lay on his back on the cavern floor, flopping like a fish.

Quick as a flash Mayhew picked up one of the dropped spears and with it swept aside the two that were menacing his black friend.

"Seize a spear, Moorfi," he shouted, "and come on."

With that, he charged upon the prostrate spider. Now was the chance to rid the world of that menace.

BUT TIRIO leaped between them and warded off the spear-thrust with his sword, at the same time calling upon the two remaining spearmen to rally to the defense of their master.

Seeing that there were three persons who did not fear the epileptic seizure, they obeyed, and Mayhew was beaten back. Moorfi joined him, but they were no match for two experienced spears and one sword. And, in response to Tirio's shouts, others of the yellow spearmen began to drift timidly back.

Seeing that he and his black friend would soon be out-numbered and overpowered, Mayhew drew back his spear-arm and cast his spear at the convulsively twitching body of the hunchback. In spite of his inexperience with such weapons, it sped true, and struck a point against the breast of the little black form. But that was all. It bounced back without penetrating, and clattered to the ground.

Snatching up another spear, and realizing the futility of further attack upon the invulnerable Spider, Mayhew called to Moorfi, and they fled together into the surrounding shadows.

Several spearmen started to pursue them, but Tirio called them back to guard their fallen master, warning them that the two fugitives might circle and return to the attack from some unexpected quarter. Thus spoke the cautious coward that was Tirio.

But such a plan was farthest from Mayhew's intentions. Having failed to slay the Spider, his chief concern now was to get out of these caves and bring word to the Muians of the Spider's plan to flood the fires.

Mayhew was well acquainted with the way out of the caves, ending in the spiral shaft which led to the surface. In fact, that was the only route, other than the globe of worluk smoke, by which he had ever left the caves. For the first several hundred yards it ran straight, and then made a sharp bend to the right, thereafter following a rather sinuous course.

So Mayhew and Moorfi raced together down this first section. The turn ahead was dimly illumined, and when they rounded it on the run they could see a flickering light reflected on the wall ahead. Evidently some one with a torch was preceding them down the tunnel.

From time to time, as he and Moorfi proceeded cautiously on, Mayhew would glance back over his shoulder. At first there were no signs of pursuit; but, by the time the fugitives had traversed about half the distance from the caves of the fires of Pele to the shaft which led upward to the outer air, there were flickering reflections of lights to be seen behind, as well as ahead.

THERE WAS but one thing to do. As between being caught by the pursuing party, and catching up with the party ahead, the latter was preferable by far.

"Better the devil we don't know than the devil we know," said Mayhew. "Come on, Moorfi."

So they rapidly quickened their pace, until on rounding a turn in the tunnel they saw ahead of them two spider-men carrying torches. Lithely and silently Mayhew and Moorfi rushed these two men. The unexpected attack succeeded. Both spider-men were seized before either of them had time to drop his torch and draw his sword.

"Silence!" cautioned the American. "Not a word out of either of you, or we'll run you through. Now hurry to the exit."

The four of them reached the open air on the starlit mountainside just as the lights of the pursuing force of spider-men appeared at the foot of the shaft.

Mayhew seized the torches of his two captives and flung them into the depths. Then he and Moorfi took off the sword-belts of the two men and buckled them onto themselves.

"Back into the shaft," he commanded, "and, as you value your lives, don't tell any one that we went west."

"West?" asked his black friend incredulously, for the Golden City lay east.

"Yes, west, of course," Mayhew replied, giving him a nudge. "Come on." And he started westward across the rocks.

Silhouetted against the starlit sky, he could see the heads of the two yellow men peering at him over the top edge of the shaft, and he knew that they could likewise see him and Moorfi silhouetted against that self-same sky. So he ran lightly over the barren rocks due west, until a dip in the terrain hid the shaft-mouth from his view, and by the same token hid him and Moorfi from the watchers at the shaft.

Then he circled rapidly, watching the stars like a true mariner for guidance as to his direction, until he was east of the shaft. And, as that direction was down hill from the shaft-mouth, he knew that he and his black companion were invisible. Glancing back over his shoulders he saw the pursuing horde emerge from the opening and set off on a run due west. He and Moorfi hurried on in the general direction of the City of Gold.

They reached the lowlands without mishap, and without further signs of pursuit; and proceeded, under the velvet sky and twinkling stars, toward the lights of a little village which they could see in the distance. The moon began to rise ahead of them beyond the village.

SUDDENLY THEY found their way barred by a line of figures which seemed to spring from the very earth. And each of these figures brandished a spear.

"Halt!" cried one of them. "Who are you?"

Mayhew and his companion halted.

"I am a peaceful gentleman traveling at night with his black servant," he answered. "Let us pass."

He glanced keenly up and down the line, to size up the situation—and suddenly realized that he had seen this spot before! That peculiarly gnarled willow tree flanked by a group of bushes which vaguely resembled a hen—he had seen it often before, through the crystal globe and the sphere of worluk smoke of his master the Spider. His enemy had located him!

"Follow me, Moorfi, and do as I do," he commanded in a low tone; then more loudly; "These men seem to be perfectly friendly, and I am sure will let us pass." And he began to advance upon them.

"Halt!" again commanded the spear-man most directly in front of him.

For reply Mayhew hurled his own spear, and the man went down.

"Come on, Moorfi!" he shouted, drawing his sword and leaping forward.

Moorfi followed, driving his own spear into one of the yellow men who was converging dangerously upon Mayhew.

They got through the line with only a few minor cuts, after having accounted for two more of the enemy.

Mayhew, in the lead, heard a groaning cry, "Master!" behind him; and, looking over his shoulder, saw that the faithful Moorfi was lying prone, with the haft of a spear protruding from between his shoulder blades. Instantly the American halted his mad flight and rushed back to place himself between the prostrate body of his friend and the horde of yellow men who were swarming toward it. Then they were upon him, and he went down beneath the force of their impact. Something struck him on the head, and he knew no more.

When he came to his senses again it was still night.

Mayhew's head ached and throbbed as he lay and waited for the last of the enemy to disappear; then he tried to roll over toward the prostrate body of his faithful black servant. But he could not move; he was pinned to the ground. Looking up, he saw the shaft of a spear protruding into the air from his own left breast.

CHAPTER XX

TO SAVE THE WORLD

IT IS STARTLING enough to come to one's senses after a battle, and find one's self lying on one's back impaled to the ground by an enemy spear. But it is even more startling to then realize that one feels no pain from the wound.

Mayhew gingerly reached up both hands, seized the shaft of the spear and gave it a gentle and tentative wiggle. Still no pain. He wiggled it some more, and it rubbed against the left side of his chest and the inside of his arm. Whoever had attempted to deliver the coup-de-grâce to him had in the moonlight mistaken the billowing folds of his toga for his own form, and had driven the spear in at the wrong place, thus hurting him not at all, although securely pinning him to the ground.

By dint of considerable effort he was finally able to wrench the spear free and throw it to one side. Then he crawled slowly and inconspicuously over the body of the Negro. For, so far as he knew, the Spider on his skull-topped, blood-red throne might still be intently watching this scene through his crystal-gazing globe.

The poor black man was completely still and dead. The tears welled up into Mayhew's eyes. Here had been a loyal servant, a true friend. But there was no time to dispose of the body; furthermore a burial would be far too conspicuous, with the Spider looking on. So, after reciting what few snatches he could remember from the invocation to the sun god, and the Christian litany for burial at sea, and throwing a handful of dirt upon the massive black body which would never fight again for its native Mu, Mayhew crept swiftly away. Still no sign of pursuit.

A cloud passed across the face of the moon, and instantly the young American sprang to his feet and ran—ran until the moon came out again. But by that time he believed that he had gotten far enough away from the gnarled willow and the hen-bush to be out of sight of the Spider, so he continued to run instead of dropping down and crawling onward again.

Thus at last he reached the village. Fortunately there were a few coins in the pouch which hung from the sword-belt he had taken from one of his two yellow captives. It was just about enough to pay his way to the city if he ate sparingly, so he washed at the inn, had the cut on his head dressed, slept for a few hours, and took the first elephant-stage the next morning for the Golden City.

At last he was home—and somehow this city of gold now was more his home than New Bedford, a city which seemed to have vanished off the earth.

Then he reached the ornate carved gold doors of the house of Julo. A lump of homesick joy arose in his throat as he mounted the steps and reached for the knocker. But the knocker was gone from its accustomed place, and the doors were barred and sealed.

No Julo! No home! What could have happened? His eyes misty, Mayhew stumbled down the steps.

A man was passing by, down the street. Mayhew hailed him.

"What has become of the house of Julo?"

"Sealed by the authorities," the man replied. "Try the next door on the left."

Then, with an expression on his face as though suddenly he realized that he had given too much information to the wrong person, the man hurried away.

Mayhew tried the next house, as directed. The doors swung open, and he darted eagerly forward, only to find the way barred by two black men with drawn scimitars.

"DON'T YOU know me?" Mayhew asked the men who faced him, for both of them were servants whom he recognized.

"The house of Julo in these days is not open to strangers," replied one of the blacks.

Well, at least it was the house of Julo!

"Is Julo well, and his gracious wife Marta?" Mayhew asked.

"Both are well," the Negro replied, "but strangers are not permitted to enter. Who are you, and what is your errand? Look, he wears an iron belt instead of one of gold! He is a spider-man!"

At this announcement both servants raised their scimitars. Mayhew drew his sword and fell back a pace.

Calling them both by name he exclaimed, "I am Adams Mayhew! I captured this belt in a fight with spider-men. But no more of this foolishness! Send for Julo, and let him identify me!"

"Will you hand over your sword and submit to search?" asked one of the Negroes, still incredulous.

For reply Mayhew flung his broadsword at their feet and held his arms aloft, so that they were soon satisfied that, even though he might not be the missing Adamo Mayho, he was at least completely unarmed and harmless. They led him within and sent for their master.

Julo came with his usual stately tread; but as soon as his eyes set upon Mayhew he rushed forward, flung his arms around his neck, and sobbed, "My son! My son! You have returned to me."

Mayhew was much touched, and not a little embarrassed. To relieve his confusion he announced, "I have important information for the government."

"Important though it may be," replied the kindly Julo, "I refuse to listen to a word of it until you have bathed and shaved and changed and rested. But you had better keep that square-cut beard. It will come in handy, if you ever have to return again to the caves of Pele."

Mayhew shuddered. The caves of Pele! Was he not yet through with the gruesome Spider?

Then he was led away to the showers and swimming pool.

*Chaos pursued
them as they ran*

Finally, bathed and shaved, and dressed in a clean toga, he
returned to the reception hall, to find that quite a group of
people had gathered there in his absence. But, of them all, he
saw only one. Eleria! Eleria of the blue eyes, honey-colored hair,
and cameo features.

At the sight of her he sprang forward and held out his arms;
but she shyly and sadly shook her yellow head and held out

her hand to him. And then he noticed that Porto was standing beside her. Somehow he had forgotten Porto.

But, after all, Porto was his friend; and Porto hadn't won Eleria from him—yet. So he greeted them both, and then turned and greeted Marta. He acknowledged the salutations of the rest of the group, men of high government position who had been active in organizing the recent expedition against the Spider.

Rapidly the developments of the past two days were sketched for the benefit of the newcomer.

It seemed that the Spider had again placarded the city with notices, this time announcing that he was now ready to destroy the world, but that he was willing to hold off for a little while longer in order to give the world a chance to arrange with him the terms of its surrender to him. If Mu, instead of parleying, should choose to fight, he would still withhold the final stroke so long as his own forces were victorious.

But if—which Pele forbid—the forces of Mu should triumph, then most assuredly the Spider would destroy the world.

Of course, no one believed that the Spider, for all his uncanny powers, could destroy the world, or even any appreciable part of the continent of Mu; but when Mayhew, cutting in on their narrative, explained the Spider's diabolical plan for the flooding of the eternal fires with sea-water, the crowd sobered.

Several scientists present admitted that the scheme held dire possibilities.

Then the narrative continued. Inasmuch as the authorities now knew, from information given them by Mayhew, the exact location of many of the spots which the menacing alchemist was wont to visualize in his crystal gazing-globe, they had watched and guarded those spots; and, as a result, had actually waylaid and killed many of the emissaries who had been sent through the worluk screen to post notices.

Now these places were barricaded off and guarded, and no one was permitted to go to them. This accounted for the condition in which Mayhew had found his old home upon his return.

He now checked over their list, and added several more places, including the river bank by the village of Forbosa and the gnarled willow tree on the mountainside.

Other cities throughout the empire were reported to be taking the same precautions, and a huge army was being recruited to march against the caves.

THE NEXT few weeks sped very quickly. There still were assassinations; but one by one the Spider's worluk-spots were located and were closed to him, until finally the only way in which he could distribute proclamations was to throw them through the smoke-haze into the proscribed spots; any one of his minions who had ventured through would have been instantly killed.

Mayhew was kept very busy, chiefly in checking up information about the Spider. But he managed to see quite a lot of Eleria; who, however, distributed her favors quite impartially between him and his friend and double, Porto.

Porto wasn't quite his double these days, for Porto was cleanshaven, whereas Adams Mayhew still wore his Egyptian beard, which he abominated, as preparation for a possible return to the caves.

At last the expedition, fully organized, set out. Similar forces were converging upon the mountains of Pele from every other city of the continent.

And when the advance up the actual slopes of the mountain began, great care was taken to avoid known menaces. The men advanced in widely spaced skirmish lines, so that wherever lava and gas were poured forth suddenly upon them, only a few were killed. Remembering the sad fate of the other expedition, valleys were avoided. Cliffs from which rocks might be hurled were flanked.

Occasionally an advance party would be attacked from the rear by yellow men appearing miraculously from nowhere. But, whenever this happened, the far-flung communication lines of the Muians located the worluk-spot and thereafter it was guarded night and day, and thus rendered impotent.

It was slow work, fighting inch by inch almost, up the barren mountainsides, but the steady advance continued, until one day a soldier guarding one of the worluk spots brought to headquarters a paper which he had found clutched in the hand of an enemy spearman who had suddenly materialized before him, and had been killed by him. It bore the repulsive Spider-crest, and was very brief. It said, "You win. And now I will destroy the earth."

Somehow, in their intentness on their steady advance, every one had forgotten the threat that victory meant destruction.

A hurried council was held, in the midst of which a steady drone in the sky began and became louder and louder as it approached. It was one of the huge mechanical dragonflies of the priesthood of Ra.

All conversation ceased, for these airships, although well known, were seldom seen, and the uncanny thought of man being able to fly always filled the bystanders with awe and dread of the supernatural.

The machine in question landed near the group, and Grand High Priest Alvo alighted from it and joined them. He had come to bless their cause.

And suddenly the arrival of the venerable prelate gave Adams Mayhew an idea.

"How many men will that flying machine hold?" he asked.

"Six, besides the driver," was the reply.

"Could it land in the mountains?"

"It can land anywhere."

QUICKLY HE sketched his plan. It was to pick out the five best swordsmen in the expeditionary forces, and then fly them and Mayhew to the mouth of the shaft which led down into the heart of the mountains. Mayhew could direct them through the tunnels, while the flying machine flew back and forth bringing more and yet more reenforcements. Perhaps in this way they could reach the dam which held back the tides of ocean from the-eternal fires of Pele, before the Spider caused this dam to be blasted away.

Alvo assented and the first squad was gathered, and hastily clambered into the silver body of the huge dragon-fly. Brave men though they were, their faces paled as, with a deafening roar, the thing left the ground.

To Mayhew the actual fact that he was flying probably seemed more truly remarkable than to the native Muians, but he did not have their superstitious dread of it. To them it represented the work of supernatural and uncanny forces controlled by the priesthood, and was on a par with the worluk of the Spider.

Accordingly Mayhew was the first to recover from that sinking feeling in the pit of the stomach which the departure from the ground had given them. He glanced over the side at the sun-kissed field, and noted that they seemed to be a blue-green, rather than the customary yellow-green when viewed from the ground. The houses seemed garishly painted blocks of wood. The rivers and ponds were black, instead of silver-blue. The whole scene below reminded him of a toy village which he had once owned as a child, with tinted excelsior for grass.

And when the flying machine bent to the wind—or so Mayhew from his nautical experience conceived it—the toy landscapes below seemed to tip and slide up to one side, while the ship of the air kept an even keel.

In a minute or two they were over the foothills and nosing sharply up toward the heights. Mayhew seized a speaking tube—he knew what they were, for he had seen them running from bridge to engine room on steamboats—and directed the navigator of the flying machine toward the opening of the shaft which was their destination.

But as he drew near it he was surprised to see a crowd of several hundred spider-men congregated there. This introduced a complication. Perhaps the Spider, through his uncanny spy system, had already learned of their venture, and had laid his plans to anticipate them.

If so, however, his plans were vain; for as the flying machine swooped down, these minions of the enemy scattered in every direction, and scuttled off over the rocks in very evident abject terror.

The space around the shaft was now practically deserted. Not completely deserted, however; for there, on a wooden replica of the red-marble skull-topped throne of the caves below, sat the Spider, squat and hunched and repulsive, croaking out orders which were not even being heard, much less obeyed.

THE AIRSHIP landed and Adams Mayhew stepped out. The five soldiers were still too mentally and spiritually shaken to accompany him; but the Spider was alone, unarmed and unguarded.

Mayhew strode over to the throne.

"Your excellency," he shouted, "at last we have you at our mercy. Quick, countermand your order to destroy the world. If not, I shall have to kill you."

A crafty grin spread over the hook-nosed face.

"And how can I send the order, Adamo Mayho," the creature croaked, "since you have scattered all my faithless followers?"

"Give me your signet ring as a token," the American replied, "and I will take your message."

"And if I refuse?"

"Then I shall have to kill you, take the ring by force, and compose my own message."

"Mayho," said the Spider fiercely, "you forget that I am invulnerable."

"And you forget that you yourself once told me that the secret of your invulnerability lies only in a certain shirt which you wear beneath your black jersey jacket. But come! No more temporizing! Give me the ring and the message!"

Mayhew began to draw his sword. But he never finished.

The creature's left hand suddenly gripped the arm of the throne, his body stiffened, and his right arm with fingers

extended shot out toward Adams Mayhew. A surge of disembodied force seemed to strike the young man squarely on the
chest, staggering him backward a pace and paralyzing his will.

"I am still master here," hissed the Spider triumphantly. "And
now you will do as I command."

"Yes, master," said Mayhew's voice, in a singsong sleep-walk-
ing tone. He did not consciously say the words; in fact he strove
to hold them back; but they came out in spite of him.

"Good!" ejaculated the Spider, a crooked smile playing across
his thin lips. "And now," he exulted, "at last I have the ship of
the air, for which I tried to bargain with the Grand High Priest.
With it I can fly to safety."

By this time the five soldiers and the pilot had gotten out of
the flying machine and were approaching the throne.

But Mayhew suddenly found a stronger will than his own
speaking through his mouth, "You five soldiers hurry down
into that shaft, where you will await me at the bottom. This is a
situation which I prefer to handle myself. And you, navigator,
come over here."

With some grumbling and uncertainty the soldiers departed
for the shaft and the pilot approached the throne.

Out shot the Spider's other hand, and he held two men by
his will, instead of one.

Mayhew's brain raced madly, thinking clearly in a detached
sort of way, but totally unable to control either his speech or his
actions. If only another of the Spider's epileptic fits would come
on. But no such luck. That had saved him once. Too much of a
coincidence to expect that it would save him again.

The Spider was speaking to the pilot, "Draw your sword and
kill Adamo Mayho. Then pick me up and carry me to your ship.
It is my will."

The bemused pilot started to draw.

CHAPTER XXI

THE SPIDER DIES

AS THE MUIAN aviator raised his sword under the influence of the mesmeric powers of that deformed paralytic, Mayhew was powerless to move or to protect himself. The Spider's evil eyes gleamed with revenge. But he had been too eager for his vengeance; he should have waited just a few minutes more.

For the five soldiers had not quite yet reached the shaft-mouth, and one of them happened to glance back. And then things began to happen. This soldier was a skillful swordsman, and a knife thrower as well, and in an instant his keen blade was hurtling through the air, straight at the luckless pilot.

But the Spider too saw the weapon coming, and exerted his will to cause the pilot to step to one side. The sword missed its mark by a hairbreadth and went clattering off down the rocks. However, the side-stepping of the pilot saved Mayhew from his blow; and before the Spider could will the man back again to the attack the five soldiers were upon him.

Swiftly moved the hypnotically fluttering fingers as the evil creature swept them all into his power. The unfortunate pilot had been killed in the onslaught, but in his place the Spider now had five new automatons to do his bidding.

However, in all the excitement and flurry and difficulty of directing his will upon five different men at once, the Spider must have forgotten to keep Adams Mayhew under control. At all events, the young American suddenly felt his own efforts for freedom bear fruit.

With a gasp he wrenched his feet free from the spell which bound them. Then drew his sword and drove it into the throat of the menace of Mu.

As the creature died, its eyes turned pitifully toward its slayer, the man whom it had once trusted and befriended; and Mayhew felt a momentary pang of disloyalty. Then he remembered the crimes of which the Spider had been guilty, and the even grosser crimes which the Spider had contemplated; and his pity and self-condemnation were changed to wild exultation.

There still was time to save the world!

Snatching off the signet ring of the dying Spider, Mayhew shouted to the five soldiers, now out of their trance again, to bring torches from the plane. Then the six of them rushed toward the opening of the caves. Their entrance was unopposed.

As they rushed through the dark corridors, with their flaring torches held aloft, the thought kept echoing in Mayhew's ears, "There still is time!"

At last they reached the spot where the excavations of the Spider had left only one thin wall of rock between the waters of the ocean and the fires of Pele. A squad of workers, led by an overseer, were just hurrying away from the scene. Mayhew rushed up to them.

Holding out the hand which bore the signet ring of the Spider, he shouted, "By the orders of his excellency, the explosion must stop."

"Back! Back!" replied the foreman. "It is too late."

With a frightful roar in that confined space, the retaining wall crumbled. The overseer and his squad dashed by, and Mayhew and his five men turned and followed. Pele and Ocean had been joined!

BEHIND THEM could be heard a deafening hissing. The whole cave filled with steam. And then an ever growing chaos of explosions began to occur behind them, increasing in frequency and intensity. The ground shook beneath their feet as they ran. The walls heaved and buckled. Pieces of ceiling fell.

The crescendo of explosions by now had merged into one continuous roar, like that of a tropical thunderstorm. Crevasses opened, which they had to jump.

And then with a showering avalanche of rock the entire passageway collapsed in front of them, completely barring the way. They were trapped in the crumbling caves of Pele!

Like madmen, Mayhew's five companions flung themselves frantically against the barrier.

But he shouted to them above the din, "Come back! There must be other ways out of this mountain. Keep your heads, men. We're not whipped until we're dead. Come on! Let's find a way."

So back they rushed again. Back toward the turmoil which was causing all this disaster.

They met a group of fleeing, terror-crazed spider-men. Mayhew stopped these newcomers, exhibited his signet of authority, calmed them, and informed them that the tunnel was barred.

"Tolofo," said one of the yellow men, "I know a detour back to the throne room. From there, there are other little-used passages leading to the surface."

"Lead on!" commanded "Tolofo."

Upon arriving at the throne room they found it and the surrounding caves packed with struggling, jostling, yellow humanity. And, in their midst, the centurion Tirio, vainly striving to calm them and learn some way of escape out of that crumbling roaring chaos.

As Adams Mayhew strode into the throne room at the head of his little group, Tirio shouted, "Seize him! Seize the impostor, in the name of his excellency!"

But Mayhew held up the signet ring and replied, "What right have you to speak for his excellency? Behold the seal of your master! I am in command here. Ho, men, seize and bind the centurion!"

But one of the five Muian soldiers who had accompanied

Mayhew had no more sense than to add, "Anyway, the Spider is dead."

A hush fell over the jostling crowd.

"In which case," shouted Tirio, "you stole the ring."

The sullen spider-men glanced from one to the other of the two men who claimed their leadership. It was a toss-up as to which the fickle mob would throw its support.

But before they could decide, Mayhew held up his hand and said, "A truce, O Tirio. All ways out must be barred, or you and this throng would not still be here. The mountain is cracking and trembling. I alone can save us."

"How?" sneered Tirio.

"By worluk. Let me mount the throne, and I will get you out of here. Not only out of here, but far from this mountain and its menace."

"Agreed!" shouted the centurion, clapping his hands in command. "Quick! Bring worluk powder!"

It was pure bluff on Mayhew's part; for, although under the tutoring of the evil alchemist he had mastered the art of crystal gazing, he never yet had made worluk.

NEVERTHELESS, WITH an assumed air of confidence, he ascended the skull-topped blood-red throne and concentrated his gaze on the little globe of glass.

"What do you see?" anxiously asked Tirio, taking up a position beside the throne.

"The public square of the Golden City," Mayhew replied, "roped off and heavily guarded."

"I can send my troops through and overwhelm them."

"You won't be given the chance," Mayhew coolly replied. "I'm the Spider now, and there's not going to be any more fighting."

He swept the vision away with a wave of his hand, and concentrated again.

"Ah, that is better," said he. "The courtyard of Julo's house, and only a small guard. I'll send some white men through first, to explain the situation to them."

By this time the bowl of worluk powder had been brought and lighted. Mayhew waved his hand imperiously; and to his own intense surprise, the ascending smoke promptly took on a globular form.

The room heaved and shook, the torches quivered and smoked, and the din of volcanic explosions and splintering rock had by now become almost deafening. Yet, by a supreme effort of his will, Mayhew held steady the ball of worluk smoke. It cleared, and Julo's courtyard could be seen by all. The throng rushed toward it.

"Back!" shouted Mayhew above the din. "Any one who attempts to penetrate the smoke screen without my permission will vanish."

The superstitious yellow men promptly edged away.

"Now," he commanded, "you five Muian soldiers go through, and explain the truce."

With blanched faces they obeyed. They could be seen talking with the guards, then staring back with unseeing bewilderment. Mayhew ordered a yellow spear-man through, and saw the man enter the courtyard unmolested.

"Your turn, Tirio," he announced.

The centurion clenched his fists and steeled himself to step through into safety. Then, in single rank, the survivors of the forces of the Spider poured into the ball of smoke.

The ceiling of the throne room began to disintegrate. The heat became oppressive, the air so sulphurous that Mayhew could hardly breathe.

A hissing, sizzling sound could be heard on his left. Mayhew did not turn to gaze from the globe of smoke before him, but out of the corner of his eye he could see the front edge of a sluggish river of lava enter through one of the doorways and slowly approach the throne.

Only a handful of yellow men remained. And then Mayhew

suddenly remembered something which the Spider had once told him: "And even if I were not a cripple, I could not hold the ball of worluk smoke intact while I myself passed through it."

Mayhew had saved the others by means of his Spider-taught mystic powers. He himself was trapped in the caves of Pele!

The last yellow man passed through. Mayhew leaned back on the throne, relaxing slightly, and sighed. Then the wall behind him collapsed, hurling him forward onto the floor and into the fast-vanishing worluk sphere.

CHAPTER XXII

CHAOS!

WHEN MAYHEW CAME to his senses again he lay securely bound on the stone flagging of Julo's courtyard. The ground trembled slightly from distant earthquake shocks. Above him stood Tirio, leering down at him.

"Thank you for getting me out of the caves of Pele," said the rat-faced centurion. "And it may interest you to know that you've enabled me to do what I've always tried to persuade the Spider to attempt—attack the Muians from the rear by means of worluk. I am now the master of the Golden City."

Mayhew groaned.

"Fool!" he said. "Mu is being racked to pieces by volcanic upheavals, yet you still prate of war and mastery. I thought that we had declared a truce."

"The truce is off," Tirio succinctly announced, as he turned on his heel and left the courtyard.

Under heavy guard Mayhew was placed in one of the bedrooms of the house which faced toward the west, toward the mountains of Pele, smoking ominously in the distance. The mountain and the land around it seemed to tremble and heave.

Then, as Mayhew gazed, there burst forth in the midst of this scene a tiny flame, which spread and grew and mounted, until it became a mighty roaring pillar of fire, several miles in diameter, and rising to the clouds.

These clouds changed to black smoke, which overshadowed the entire land and became shot with many lightnings, blending strangely with the red glare of the pillar of fire. Then from the northward a tidal wave rushed across the intervening space. The house began to rock and shake.

The setting sun appeared beneath the pall of smoke and lingered upon the horizon like a ball of fire, red and angry looking. And well might he be angry at the devastation which Pele, the bride whom he had scorned, was wreaking upon his beloved land.

For a while the sun-god lingered to watch the holocaust which he was powerless to avert; then, as though with a shrug of resignation, he sank beneath the waves. Deep dark night, lit by the hell-fires of Pele and the silver flashes of lightning, settled over land and sea.

During the night most of what was left of Mu was torn asunder and rent to pieces. The central pillar of fire died down, its force spent; but in all directions could be seen and heard the flash and roar of many relatively small explosions, each destroying forever a section of the land.

Down, down sank the continent of Mu into the eternal fires of Pele; and as it sank, the seas rushed in and overwhelmed it, causing more explosions as the water seeped into the volcanic pits.

When morning came—when Ra rose once more from the sea, redder even than on the evening before—he disclosed a steaming, smoking expanse of waves beneath a sky of crimson-tinted, billowing smoke. The Golden City alone stood intact. Here and there in the distance, island peaks projected from the sea; and occasionally huge bubbles, miles in extent, would belch upward. The water was thick with mud, and the air was so filled with sulphur fumes as to be almost unbreathable.

Then the sun passed upward into the overhanging pall of smoke and the whole surface of the deep was plunged into night once more.

DURING THE night and day and night of horror, Mayhew remained under guard. Food was brought him from time to time. Occasionally he slept. But his captors refused to tell him any news of what was going on in the city.

On the second morning his double, Porto, was thrust, battered and bleeding, into his cell. It seems that Porto with some others of the army had fled to their ships when the eruption had started. The tidal wave had swept them close to the Golden City. There they had landed, to be immediately set upon by the forces of Tirio, whom they unexpectedly found to be in control. Porto and a few others had been captured. The rest scattered.

Later in the morning Mayhew and Porto were led out of the house, through the streets, and into the public square. The streets were nearly deserted, but the square was thronged with yellow men, thugs of Tirio, and a few miscellaneous Muians. Tirio sat in state on a golden throne, and by his side stood Eleria, her hands bound.

"The heavenly twins have come to see you, my dear," bantered Tirio, indicating Mayhew and Porto with a wave of his hand. "And now I have a proposition to put to you. You have declined the honor of becoming my queen. You have very bravely refused to yield to threats, and for that display of courage I love you all the more. So now I am going to buy your love, and at the same time get a little fun out of watching your choice. If you will agree to marry me peacefully and willingly, I will spare the life of one of your two friends. Which one shall it be?"

"You will spare him, in return for my promise?" asked the girl.

"Well, not exactly. But if you marry me, I give you my word of honor that he shall then go free. Which of the twins is it to be?"

"Honor?" contemptuously replied Eleria. "You do not know what it is."

The rat face went white, and Porto and Mayhew both smiled grimly.

"Wipe that grin off!" shrieked Tirio, and two attendants slapped them across their mouths.

Eleria then said conciliatingly, "I am sorry, Tirio, that I spoke so hastily, but I have suffered much and am not alto-

*The ground
heaved so that
they could
scarcely keep
their feet. All
about them
buildings
toppled and were
crushed to earth*

gether responsible for what I say. Let me make you a counter proposition. Release both of them, and I will marry you gladly and willingly."

"No!" cried the two prisoners in unison, and Mayhew added, as his eye lighted on a small object on the ground in front of him. "We can take care of ourselves."

Tirio by this time had regained his composure.

"You think so?" he sneered. "And how do you propose to take care of yourself, Adamo Mayho?"

The crowd guffawed.

"If you weren't a coward, you'd come down off that throne and fight me," Mayhew replied. "I'll fight you with swords, at which you are reputed an expert. Or I'll fight you with my bare hands the way I did that day on the wharves over a year ago."

There were several snickers in the crowd, and Tirio stiffened. Then he grinned diabolically. He knew how to turn this into a joke and thus appeal to his followers.

"I tell you what," he said. "Were it not for my duty to these men who have chosen me to rule over them, I would gladly risk my life to settle old scores with you on even terms. But I'll give you a chance. Fight me as you are, but with my having a sword, and let the winner take the girl. What say you?"

"I'll do it!" said the American with surprising eagerness. "But what guarantee will you give that you will go through with the bargain if I win?"

Tirio was a bit taken back by this ready acceptance of his preposterous offer. But his confusion was covered up by Porto's asking: "Where do I come in on this?"

"Oh, if you wish, you can fight the winner," Tirio declaimed with an airy wave of the hand. "Well, let's get going."

"No! No!" begged Eleria. "Don't kill them. I'll marry you."

"You'll do that, anyway," asserted Tirio grimly. "On with the fight!"

He stepped down from his throne and began to draw his sword.

"Just a minute," hastily interposed Mayhew. "My sandal is untied."

Dropping to one knee, he tugged at the leather thong. It came loose. Then picking up something else, he arose to his feet.

Round and round his head Mayhew swung his right arm. Tirio stared, his sword half-drawn.

Mayhew's arm suddenly ceased its gyrations and lashed out toward his enemy. The leather thong fluttered from Mayhew's hand.

Tirio's sword clattered to the cobblestones and he slumped into a soundless heap, while blood streamed from a cut on his forehead. Mayhew's childhood practice with a sling, years ago in New Bedford, had not been in vain.

For a moment every one, including the victor, stood motionless. Then an angry growl broke from the crowd. But the sound was drowned in another growl, as the earth began to tremble and shake. A few bricks fell into the square. The surrounding buildings began to totter. Panic stricken, the crowd fled.

Mayhew snatched up Tirio's sword and cut Eleria's bonds, and the three friends hastened away.

The ground heaved so that they could scarcely keep their feet. All about them buildings were crashing to earth. It was a miracle that they got out of the city alive.

At last they dragged themselves onto a little hill on the outskirts and gazed back at what was left of the once proud Golden City, now an indescribable chaos of fallen masonry, sprinkled with fires. But the fires were short-lived, for the city was settling fast, and even as the fugitives gazed, the sea swept in and engulfed it all.

The Golden City was no more.

Several hundred survivors occupied the hill, now an island, and among these survivors they found Julo and Marta. Then night fell.

IN THE lurid red light of the volcanic morning, Julo instinctively took command of the little community. A small boat had drifted ashore in the night. It turned out to be equipped and provisioned.

Julo said, "Two of us must take this boat, search for the nearest undestroyed land, and send back help. And, even if help should fail to reach us, two of us will at least have been saved. Let us draw lots. The winner can choose his companion."

So the drawing was held, and Adams Mayhew won.

"I choose Eleria," he promptly said.

But she sadly shook her head as she replied, "No, Adamo dear. You are my very best friend in all the world; but, if you will forgive me, I will stay here with Porto, whom I love." And she put her hand through Porto's arm.

Mayhew gulped, then turning to Julo, asked, "Is the lot transferable?"

"I don't know why not."

"Then I transfer it to my good friend Porto, and to his bride."

So Porto and Eleria were duly married at high noon by the magistrate Julo, according to the ritual of Ra, and they set forth that same day in the little boat. A gentle wind bore them steadily westward and Adams Mayhew watched with aching heart until their boat was a mere speck on the horizon.

Long after all the others had left the shore and gone inland, Mayhew sat on the beach and stared moodily at the western horizon, which concealed his two friends. The tide rose, and he moved away from it. Then he noticed that the tide seemed to be rising with unusual speed.

Faster and faster came the waters. Mayhew left the shore and scrambled up the hill. And then it dawned on him that the trouble was not that the waters were rising. On the contrary, the land was settling!

Horrified, he ran to warn his friends, though what good a warning would do them he did not stop to consider.

But the warning was never delivered. The land heaved, and cracked, and threw him to his knees. The sea reached in and engulfed him and swept him away, whirling him over and over, blinding and choking him. Madly he fought his way to the surface; and at last he made it, and lay there spitting and coughing and drawing deep breaths of air into his tortured lungs.

Then he looked around him. The island and all his friends were gone! He was alone in the midst of the Pacific Ocean!

But in the western distance there rose from the horizon a thin column of smoke. This smoke steadily approached him, until he could see the steamer from which it emanated. The steamer bore down upon him. He waved and shouted. The steamer stopped and lowered a boat.

When he was safely aboard the first questions were in a strange tongue which no one could understand. Then some one asked him in English for his name.

He told them: "Adams Mayhew of the whaling barque Alaska."

"Shipwrecked?"

"No. Fell overboard."

"When?"

"September, 1891."

At which there were many significant glances, and one man exclaimed, "But, my dear fellow, this is 1932!"

"Where have you been all this while?" asked some one else sarcastically.

"On the continent of Mu," he replied with open-faced simplicity.

"Oh, you've been reading one of Col. Churchward's books. Mu was destroyed by earthquakes and sank beneath the waves *twenty-five thousand* years ago!"

Adams Mayhew had never heard of Churchward; but he deemed it best to keep the story of his adventure to himself, until he found a sympathetic listener in me.

A MYSTERIOUS DISAPPEARANCE

THERE IS A surprising amount of factual basis to "The Golden City." There actually was such a whaling barque as the Alaska. She did arrive in San Francisco Bay on November 8, 1891; and the entire account of her crew seeing the vision of the golden city is absolutely and literally true, even to the extent of the Alaska's approaching close enough to the wharves so as to make out the individual features of the inhabitants. No city which existed in 1891 fits the description.

Captain Fisher of the Alaska was my uncle. So was Tisdale S. Pease, a member of the crew, from whom I have often heard the story.

Adams Mayhew actually fell overboard earlier in the voyage, in 1889; but I took the literary license of combining the two episodes.

For my knowledge of the lost continent of Mu, I am indebted to the researches of Col. Churchward. The shape of North America at the time of Mu, is in accord with contemporary maps discovered by Col. Churchward; also with geological data in the hands of the U.S. Department of the Interior.

May I express my thanks to Lyn Fox (City Editor of the San Francisco *Chronicle*), Miss Mary Aloysia Byrne (of the reference room of the San Francisco Public Library), Miss Mabel R. Gillis (California State Librarian), and my classmate, Felix T. Smith, for their assistance in checking up my facts.

Ralph Milne Farley.

ABOUT THE AUTHOR

THE IDENTITY OF Ralph Milne Farley is shrouded in mystery. When his first story, "The Radio Man," appeared in the *Argosy—All-Story Weekly*, in 1924, it was announced editorially that the author was the world's leading authority in two lines, to name either of which would be instantly to reveal his identity.

"The Radio Man" attracted considerable attention and comment in literary and technical circles, and one newspaper, the Boston *Post*, even put one of its best sleuth-hounds on the trail. By careful study of the internal evidence in the story, especially the fact that the narrative started on Chappaquiddick Island, off the coast of Massachusetts, and that the hero was described as a member of the Harvard class of 1909, the *Post* narrowed the field to two Harvard '09 men who own estates on the island in question: namely, Dr. Francis M. Rackermann and former State Senator Roger Sherman Hoar. Dr. Rackemann is a recognized authority on hay-fever and eczema; whereas Senator Hoar has written the outstanding American texts on "Constitutional Conventions" and on "Ballistics."

Recently apropos Farley's "The Radio Flyers," the Boston *Post* announced that further evidence, namely a similarity between certain passages in one of Farley's stories and a whimsy entitled "Blue Dandelions," published years ago by Senator Hoar in the *Atlantic Monthly*, definitely establishes their identity. The *Post* ought to know, as Hoar used to work for them.

So we are accepting this verdict, and are publishing the portrait of the Senator.

Ralph Milne Farley

Hon. Roger Sherman Hoar (alias Ralph Milne Farley), was born in Waltham, Massachusetts, on April 8, 1887. Until eight years ago he lived in Concord, Massachusetts.

He holds three degrees from Harvard University. In addition to his service in the State Senate, he has been Assistant Attorney General of Massachusetts, and Legal Advisor of the Constitutional Convention of 1917. He resigned that position to enlist as a private at the outbreak of the World War. Rapidly rising to captain, he served as senior instructor in military surveying at the Coast Artillery School, and later on the Technical Staff.

After the war, Bucyrus Company, of South Milwaukee, Wisconsin, the largest manufacturer of excavating machinery in America, was looking for a combined lawyer and engineer to take charge of their legal affairs, and persuaded Captain Hoar to resign his commission. He is now the attorney of their successor, Bucyrus-Erie Company. On the side, he is Lecturer in Physics at Marquette University, and a reserve major of the Technical Staff of the United States Army.

Major Hoar is the author of a number of works on law and engineering, and is a contributor to legal and technical magazines.

He is the inventor of several patented devices," including the north-finding apparatus used by his hero, *Eric Redmond,* in "The Radio Flyers." This is an actual practical instrument, useful in aiming big guns, the patent to which is owned by the War Department.

His chief interests, outside his official position, are his family, higher mathematics, blue dandelions and writing.

He is married, has a daughter and two sons, and lives in South Milwaukee.

Although each of his titles contains the word "Radio," he has never owned a radio set. No item of the technical background of any of his stories has ever been successfully challenged.

THE ARGOSY™ LIBRARY

THE BEST FICTION
FROM THE FRANK
A. MUNSEY LINE

www.ingramcontent.com/pod-product-compliance
Lightning Source LLC
Chambersburg PA
CBHW050533260626
47157CB00004B/1582